TOUCH AND GO

GRAHAM SHARPE

A Sid Harta publication
This edition published in 2023 by Sid Harta Publishers,
23 Stirling Cres, Glen Waverley VIC 3150, Australia

Copyright © Graham Sharpe 2023
Cover design and typesetting: Luke Harris, WorkingType Studio

ISBN: 978-1-922958-39-6
pp278

ABOUT THE AUTHOR

Graham Sharpe has led an adventurous life, starting when he served with a "crack" special forces battalion and army intelligence unit. He has travelled the world extensively, lived in several countries and worked for organisations  varying in size from multinationals, where he rose to be managing director and chief executive, to his own small company, where he was everything from chairperson to "chief bottle washer". Now he lives quietly, having been widowed, after many years of marriage to "the most gorgeous girl in the world!".

ALSO BY THE AUTHOR

The Kenyan bush is breathtakingly beautiful but potentially deadly without the honed skills of a highly trained marksman and experienced "white hunter". Gavin has all the skills needed to run his highly regarded safari company, but does he have the skills to deal with the additional challenges thrown at him whilst on safari with Sir William and his beautiful wife? The unexpected just keeps happening...

He exploded through the scrub like an express train out of hell...
MOONLIGHT PREDATOR
GRAHAM SHARPE

My daughter, Belinda, for acting as my literary agent and for introducing me to Kerry and the excellent team at Sid Harta Publishing. And to Jenn Zabinskas, my editor, for your support and encouragement.

DISCLAIMER

This novel's story and characters are fictitious. Although certain long-standing institutions, agencies and public offices are mentioned, the characters and situations involved are wholly imaginary.

GLOSSARY

SAS   Special Air Services

MC   Military Cross

DSO   Distinguished Service Order

SOE   Special Operations Executive

IRA   Irish Republican Army

As the train pulled out of Oxford Station, Caroline settled herself into the corner seat of her first-class compartment. Once again, she wondered who Sir Alastair Brown was, whom he represented, and why he had invited her to meet him at his Victoria Street office. She supposed he must be involved with the press and, with luck, he was going to commission her to write a feature on something or other. In any case, why worry, a day in London with all expenses paid couldn't be bad. It amazed her how lucky she was, that after only two years as a freelance features writer she had become recognised to the extent that feature editors were actually asking her to write stuff. Bit of a change from the early days when she had to spend so much time just "knocking on doors" trying to get work published. How proud John would have been of her.

She looked across the compartment at the only other passenger, a smartly dressed older man, who, though he was pretending to read *The Times*, had obviously been studying her. This didn't surprise, or worry, her, as she was used to it; people were always aware of her. She let the short skirt of her red Armani suit ride a little further up her long, slender thigh. Her companion cleared his throat and disappeared into the enveloping environs of *The Times*.

Caroline smiled to herself; it was wonderful to feel alive again after the last two years. She was even beginning to be physically interested in the opposite sex again; wonder upon wonder, she had almost given up hope of ever getting clear of the mire of her sadness. It was a strange thing but she knew that her revival was mainly due to the awful, humiliating, degrading experience she had had a couple of months ago, in an Arab embassy, at the hands of that abominable man called Billy Grant. Ugh! She hoped she never saw him again.

She took a cab from the station and arrived at Sir Alastair's address at the appointed time of eleven-thirty. There wasn't a nameplate on the door to say what organisation it was, and she had to use a security speaker to say whom she was, and whom she was visiting. The door was opened by a formidably large commissionaire in a blue uniform and cap who handed her over to a grey-haired, middle-aged secretary to take up to Sir Alastair. Sir Alastair walked across his very impressive room to greet Caroline and showed her to a leather armchair, in a sitting area, well away from his desk.

'It's so kind of you to come to see me Mrs Dalglish, particularly at such short notice. Will you have some coffee or a drink of some kind?' he asked in what Caroline always thought of as a "cigars and port" type of voice.

'I'd love some coffee.'

'Good. Did you have a pleasant journey up from Oxford? Such a nice city. I have fond memories of it from my undergrad days, that was, of course, rather a long time ago. Whereabouts do you live, actually in the city?'

'I have a house in the Crescent, Park Town.'

'I know, off the Banbury Road, very grand.'

'It certainly is for me; it was my husband's.'

'Ah yes, of course. I remember his tragic death, such a loss, he was a brilliant man and one of our greatest historians. It must be some two years ago now; it was a road accident if I remember rightly?'

'Yes, as always he must have been thinking about something else when he was riding his bike to a meeting at Merton; he rode down The Turl and, without looking, straight out into the High where he was hit, and killed instantly by a bus.'

Caroline was surprised that she was at last able to say this without tears coming into her eyes, but she was glad that the coffee arrived at that moment. As she sipped her coffee, she looked at Sir Alastair who was a slim, good-looking man in, she guessed, his late sixties, and wondered when he was going to tell her why he had asked her to come and see him.

He must have read her mind as he said, 'I expect, Mrs Dalglish, that you wonder who I am and why I asked to see you? Firstly, let me tell you who I am; I'm a sort of press liaison officer for the Government. The reason I've asked you here today, Mrs Dalglish, is that there is a feature we would possibly like you to write for us; however, before I go on, I need some answers from you. Firstly, would you be prepared to commit several weeks to one project? Secondly, would you be prepared to spend some of that time in San Francisco? Thirdly, would you be prepared to accept, however much you do or do not write, one thousand pounds per week, plus all expenses? Fourthly, are you against the use of narcotic drugs? And the fifth and last question: would you be prepared to be exposed to a certain amount of danger?'

Caroline sat for a minute, thinking to herself, *what on earth is this all about? If this man is a press liaison officer, then I'm a Dutchman.* To the first three questions she thought the answers easy—yes, yes, please. The fourth question was no problem either, but the last question, what did that mean?

'Mrs Dalglish, I don't want you to rush your answers so why don't we go and have a spot of lunch to give you time to think it over and then, when we come back, we can talk some more?'

'Yes, Sir Alastair, that would be very nice, thank you.'

A large black official-looking car took them to The Savoy, no less, where they went into the Grill Room—Sir Alastair was very well-known—Caroline laughed inwardly, *press liaison officer!*

After an excellent Dover Sole, with a glass or two of Chablis, followed by fresh fruit salad, they returned to Sir Alastair's office.

During lunch Caroline had thought about his proposition and decided she was interested but also that she wanted to know what it was really all about.

When they were seated in their armchairs in his office again, she took the bull by the horns and said, 'Sir Alastair, I'm very interested in doing this job for you and I accept your five points, but it is obvious to me that there is more in this than meets the eye. I'll require additional information such as the subject of the feature to assess whether on not it is within my capabilities.'

Sir Alastair looked at her for a few minutes without saying anything, then he leant forward and, looking straight into her clear blue eyes, asked, 'Why are you interested? Is it purely because of the money it would earn you?'

She ran a hand through her long, blonde hair, and with a half-smile, replied, 'Come, come, Sir Alastair, don't tell me you haven't checked me out well enough not to know that I earn a thousand pounds most weeks, I am very much in demand and usually get in excess of three hundred pounds for every thousand words I write. Actually, I don't even have to work at all as my husband left me well provided for. No, it's much more than money, that's why I need to know more before I make a final decision.'

It was Sir Alastair's turn to smile. 'Yes, I must agree that's the information I have. I've also been told that you're a very intelligent young lady and I must, from my own observations, also agree with that statement.'

She gave him a nod of thanks and said, 'Are you prepared to tell me more?'

'Yes, but before I do, I must ask you if you will give me your solemn word that you'll not mention any of this to anyone else.'

'Yes, of course; you have my word.'

'The feature that we wish you to write is concerning a guru, and one of these new strange sects called *The Foundation of the Divine Spirit*. Several people, including myself, are sure that this is a cover for something else and that young women are being used who are quite innocent of what is really happening. You will immediately ask why we want a feature written instead of sending in the cavalry. The reason is twofold: firstly, we don't have enough evidence to start the ball rolling, and secondly, we've got a budget squeeze, as usual, and can't spend more money than we have to. There is also, I suppose, a third reason, which one doesn't like to admit to, the fear of egg on one's face if it turns out to be absolutely nothing. As far as you're concerned, you may end up with a first-class feature, that we may or may not allow to be published depending upon the politics of the situation, or nothing at all. However, in any case, you will get your fee and expenses and perhaps a bit of excitement.'

'Will I have an appointment with the guru who will then tell me all? Seems unlikely. Or do I just fish around and try to find out what's going on? I must admit it all sounds a bit suspect, Sir Alastair.'

Caroline thought he looked a bit embarrassed as he cleared his throat. 'Perhaps I'd better fill in a bit more detail. The idea is that we put you in touch with the UK set-up and hope that they recruit you and send you to San Francisco as one of their girls. You'll then be able to follow the whole procedure at first hand. The reason we have picked you is because, firstly, you are a trained observer and secondly, if they did get onto you, they'll just think you're doing it for the story and send you away.'

'Meaning,' Caroline said sardonically, 'that if it was one of your liaison staff, these people might do something more than just send them away?'

'In a nutshell, yes.'

'It's very complimentary of you to think that these people in San Francisco are going to know, if I tell them my name, that I'm an English feature writer and that I mean them no harm. I must say, Sir Alastair, that I find that hard to believe.'

'Does this mean, Mrs Dalglish, that you are not, in the circumstances, interested in helping us?'

'I didn't say that, but I'll have to give it very careful consideration. Have you any way of giving me protection while I'm in San Francisco?'

'Yes, we have some very good arrangements for that. Do you know of William Grant?'

'William Grant?'

'Yes, the Hon. William Grant, son and heir of Lord Grant, and at the moment, chief executive of his own security company, *International Security Service*. They specialise in supplying bodyguards and security for high-risk people and conferences. We use them a lot. For instance, if you noticed the blue-uniformed chaps in our entrance hall, they're part of his organisation. His office is only just down the road. Let me call him and see if he can pop over and join us for a chat.'

As he went over to his desk to phone, Caroline asked in a somewhat subdued voice, 'He's not the one known as Billy Grant, is he?'

'Yes, that's from the old days, most people call him Billy. You know him then?'

'No, but we've met.'

As Sir Alastair started to talk on the phone, Caroline

was remembering, with a shudder, the last time she'd met Billy Grant. It had been early summer and she'd been invited to do a feature on an Arab prince who was visiting England. She was particularly good at interviewing people and this was a very prestigious assignment for her. The Prince, who was living in exile, was trying to start a counter revolution to regain control of his country with the help of certain other Arab states. He was visiting London for talks and staying at a friendly Arab embassy where Caroline had gone to meet him. When she'd arrived at the embassy, she'd noticed a lot of police activity outside but thought nothing of it. On entering the embassy she'd been asked to take a seat in the beautiful reception hall. Having her camera with her—she always thought of herself as rather a good photographer—she took a few shots of the hall. Then she was unable to resist looking through a door that opened off the hall and found it led into a magnificently furnished room; without thinking she went in to take some more photographs. Just as she was raising her camera, she was violently seized from behind and then a very large man appeared in front of her and forcibly took her camera and shoulder bag from her. Up to this time no one had said a word, but at this point she'd said very loudly, 'What the hell's going on?'

No answer. She was still held firmly from behind. The second man very gingerly looked at and opened her camera.

'Do you mind!' Caroline said. 'You'll ruin the film.'

Still no answer, complete silence. Then this same man emptied the contents of her handbag on the floor and stood looking at it for a minute before he stirred everything around with his foot.

'Good God! What do you think you're doing?' Caroline half shouted. 'Let me go at once.'

Still, no one else said anything. Then a third man came into the room and, even in those unpleasant circumstances, she couldn't help thinking how attractive he looked.

'Have you searched her?' he asked in a pleasant, modulated voice.

'No, didn't like to, boss.'

The implication was too much for Caroline and she said in an enraged voice, 'If anyone lays a hand on me, there'll be real trouble. Let me go right now.'

The third man then said, 'Okay, you two, take an arm each and hold it above her head, and I'll do the honours.'

Caroline couldn't believe what then happened; the man who had been holding her from behind came into view, he was very big and very ugly. As he stood beside her, he took her right wrist and forcefully held her arm at full stretch above her head. The man who had searched her handbag did the same thing with her left arm.

'Okay, boss.'

The third man, whom they had referred to as "boss", then stepped forward, and dropping to one knee, encircled her left ankle with his hands and then ran them to the very top of her leg.

Caroline gasped and sobbed, 'For God's sake, stop this.'

He took no notice, but just did the same to her other leg. As she'd been very brown from a recent stay in Crete, she was not wearing tights but only a flimsy pair of Charnos silk pants, which he then proceeded to run his hands over. She was wearing a navy blue spot suit so, when he finished under her skirt, his warm, firm hands moved up under her jacket and explored her bra. When he finally finished, the two gorillas, as she had begun to think of them, let go of her arms and she nearly fell. It was not so much a feeling of fear, as a feeling of outrage and humiliation. She tried to speak, but her mouth just opened and shut.

'What are you doing here and who are you?' asked the boss man.

It was a good minute before Caroline was able to answer. 'I'm Caroline Dalglish and I've been invited to do a feature on the Prince.'

'Then why are you in this apartment on your own without an ID badge?'

Before she could answer, one of the other two men stepped forward and held out the letter, taken from Caroline's bag, asking her to come to the embassy for the interview.

'Here's a letter, boss, asking Ms Dalglish to be here today.'

'How do we know you're Miss Dalglish?'

'I'm not, I'm Mrs Dalglish; please tell me your name as I intend to make as much fuss as I can about your disgraceful behaviour.'

'My name's Billy Grant. You're lucky to get off as lightly as you did. You were caught, taking photographs, in a part of the embassy that you've no right to be in. I'd also point out that you're on *foreign soil* that does not come under British jurisdiction, so if you want to make a fuss, you'll have to take it to the Arabs who, incidentally, we work for.'

He then had the impertinence to smile at her. His two henchmen also smiled and one of them picked up her bag, stuffed everything into it, including her camera, and handed it back to her. Billy Grant, as she then knew who he was, turned to the toughest looking of his two henchmen and said, 'Take Miss Dalglish out into the reception hall while I find someone to look after her. Well,' he smiled at her, 'it's been nice getting to know you.' The other two men chuckled.

At that moment Caroline decided that Billy Grant was the most hateful, chauvinistic man she'd ever come across, and that if she never met him again, it would be too soon.

When she had been back in the reception hall for a few minutes, an immaculate and very suave Arab came out to see her. He apologised for any inconvenience caused but said the whole place was in turmoil as there had been an assassination attempt on the Prince shortly before she arrived. The assassins were thought to be still in the embassy. He also said, with a charming smile, that because she was so brown a security man thought she was an Arab girl with dyed-blonde hair. It was very regrettable, he said, but he was sure she would agree, in the circumstances, quite understandable. He went on to say that the Prince had been spirited away and, therefore, the interview could not take place. The Prince and the Ambassador were very sorry and would she accept a small gift to make up for the lost interview and any inconvenience caused. She was then handed an envelope which, when she had subsequently opened it, contained two thousand pounds in English banknotes. *Very nice too,* she'd thought, but it didn't make up for being manhandled, like a girl in a slave market, by an arrogant chauvinist.

She came out of her reverie to hear Sir Alastair saying, 'Billy will be with us in a few moments. My word, look at the time. What about a cup of tea?'

Caroline was just taking her first sip of Earl Gray tea when the door opened and Sir Alastair's secretary announced the arrival of Billy Grant. Sir Alastair went forward to meet him and Caroline got up too; she wanted to be on her feet and as much on a level with him as possible when they met again. She drew herself to her full five feet six, but she decided she might just as well not have bothered as he looked down on her from well over six feet. He looked the same, but different, just as tanned and fit as before, but perhaps his dark brown, slightly wavy hair was a bit tidier than at the embassy, and his hazel eyes warmer and more relaxed. This time he was looking very well-groomed in a dark-grey, chalk-stripe suit, silk shirt and tie rather than the, sort of, para-military kit he was wearing before.

As Sir Alastair introduced them, Billy held out his hand to her, which she took reluctantly and shuddered as she felt the same smooth, warm hand that a few months previously had, uninvited, explored her body. The worst aspect, Caroline thought, was that hand actually made her feel excited and even seemed to make her blood surge through her body.

'Hello again,' Billy said, his laughing hazel eyes looking directly into her cool blue ones.

'Of course, you've met before. I was forgetting that,' said Sir Alastair.

'Only once, but that was a very short but revealing meeting. It was that business with the Arab Prince at the embassy. Mrs Dalglish revealed to me at that time what a ... um ... very cool, collected lady she is.'

Caroline glared at Billy but was at a loss for an appropriate retort.

'Now then, Billy, help yourself to a cup of tea and let's get down to business. You already know all about this guru chap in San Francisco and I've explained to Mrs Dalglish how and why she can help us. She's already asked a lot of questions which I've been able to answer and now she has asked if we're able to guarantee, or at any rate, oversee her safety while she's on this project. This is where you come in as your organisation is responsible for that aspect. I imagine you'll have someone from your company travelling with her, but undercover. Is that right, and if so, who will you appoint to the job? Michael or David, I would expect?'

'Yes, either of those would have been very suitable, but I regret that they are both tied up on assignments. There's no alternative, I'll have to undertake it myself.'

Caroline's gasp was drowned by Sir Alastair saying loudly, 'Oh! Very good, very good.'

It was the last thing Caroline wanted to do, to spend time with this awful man; she couldn't think of anything worse. It was a pity because she was beginning to be really interested in, and excited by, the thought of this San Francisco investigation. She gave Billy a cold look, then turned to Sir Alastair who was still looking pleased.

'Do you really think it's necessary for me to have a *minder*?' she asked. 'I'm quite used to looking after myself, and in any case, I'm sure there's no great risk. As you said, Sir Alastair, if they find out I'm a journalist, all they'll do is send me away.'

'Alastair, I don't think you've been fair to Miss Dal—'

'Mrs.'

'—to Mrs Dalglish if you haven't told her that there is

a distinct possibly of danger, if these people should find out that she is there to gather information and not as a follower of the guru.'

'Yes, yes. I mentioned to Mrs Dalglish this factor and that's why she asked about any security and protection arrangements.'

'I did realise that there might be some danger, but I thought that that would refer to perhaps being roughed up a little, and that does happen occasionally, even in England,' Caroline said, turning and glaring at Billy.

Billy smiled at her. 'Yes, I believe it does, and I'm sure you could take care of that, but in this case, it could be more drastic. I think, for instance, that you should be told, if you haven't already been, that two of the girls that went out to visit the guru have completely disappeared. This may not mean anything; it could be quite innocent. For instance, they could have met boys and gone off with them. On the other hand, it might be something much more sinister and this possibility shouldn't be ignored.'

Caroline *was* grateful to Billy Grant for telling her, particularly as she could tell Sir Alastair was not pleased.

'Well,' she said, 'it would appear that this is a much more serious matter than I'd realised, in which case, I will need strongarm backup.'

'Yes, I agree you most certainly will, and I'm sure, Alastair, that you agree too.'

'Yes, yes, I've thought that all along; after all, Billy, that's why you're here.'

'That's settled then,' said Caroline, 'but I don't see why Mr Grant has to come himself. He must be much too busy. Couldn't we wait until one of the others is free?'

'I do think, Mrs Dalglish, that if Billy is prepared to accompany you himself then we should take advantage of his offer. I can't think of anyone I'd rather have looking after you.'

'That's settled then, I'll accompany Mrs Dalglish. Have dates been settled yet? ... No, well as soon as they are, perhaps Mrs Dalglish and I can get together to discuss details. I'm afraid I must leave you now as I've another meeting to attend. How are you getting back to Oxford, Mrs Dalglish?'

'By train.'

'Let one of my boys drive you back. It's now well into the rush hour.'

'No, I don't want to put you to any trouble.'

'It's no trouble. He'll be waiting for you outside. I'll be in touch, Alastair. Goodbye to you both.'

Caroline watched him cross the room and thought

again what an attractive man he was and how she hated him, and all his confidence and nonchalance.

'I hadn't realised how late it is. I'm sure you must be wanting to get back to Oxford. It's a good idea, anyway, for you to think things over for a couple of days, and then I'll be in touch again and we can meet to finalise our arrangements.'

'Yes, that'll be fine. One point though, does Billy Grant really have to accompany me? Wouldn't it be better if one of his men did?'

'Oh no, if he'll do it, he's the best person you could get. He's tough, resourceful and has powerful contacts everywhere. I must admit, however, that I'm very surprised he offered. He doesn't usually do field work of this nature, and he doesn't like women.'

'He's a woman hater?'

'No, no, nothing like that, if anything the opposite. I understand that he's dated half the most beautiful women in London. No, it's just that he doesn't trust women or let them get too close to him. It all goes back to when he was six years old and his mother, the first Lady Grant, ran away with an Argentinian polo-playing beef baron. He loved his mother very much, and thought she loved him, but she didn't even say goodbye to him, nor has she seen

Billy from that day to this. Because of that he never wants to be involved with a woman in anything that necessitates his having to rely on or trust them. Very sad, and I know it upsets his father very much, as his greatest wish is for Billy to get married and return to Scotland to run the family estates. Well now, Mrs Dalglish, hadn't you better be on your way?'

A secretary saw Caroline down to the reception where the man in blue saluted her, and said, 'Your car's waiting outside, Miss Dalglish.' He indicated an all-black Range Rover with smoked-glass windows, parked on the double yellow lines with a female traffic warden, talking and laughing with the driver. The driver, whom Caroline recognised as one of the two who had been at the embassy with Billy Grant, sprang to attention. 'Good evening, Miss Dalglish, all ready to go?'

'Yes, thank you,' she said, smiling at the traffic warden and climbing into the front passenger seat.

'I'm Fred,' the driver said. 'You want to go to Oxford, is it in Oxford or on the outskirts?'

'Right in the centre, do you know the Randolph? ... Well, if you can get there, I'll direct you the rest of the way.'

Fred, his huge bulk crouched over the wheel, chatted on as he drove fast, but well, through the heavy traffic.

Suddenly he blurted out, 'We were all very sorry about what happened at the embassy, particularly the boss. It was just one of those things, it couldn't be helped.'

'I wasn't very happy about it either, but I understand.' To change the subject, she asked, 'Have you known Mr Grant long?'

'God bless you, miss, yes. I was in the army with him.'

'I didn't know he was a soldier.'

'Yes, and one of the vest. The Black Watch, which all his family have served in, and then the SAS. He won an MC in Ireland and a DSO in the Gulf War. He was a major when he left, but everyone said he would have ended up top man if he'd stayed on.'

'Why did he leave if he was so good?'

'It was because of an operation that I was on with him, which we're still not really allowed to talk about. I was one of his sergeants. Basically, we went to rescue some political hostages, including women and children, and suddenly there was a change of allegiance and we were told to leave them to their fate. That just wasn't the boss, so he got them out anyway. He was reprimanded and returned to his regiment in semi-disgrace; so, he quit. In fact, I don't think he would have stayed much longer anyway, he'd just about had his fill of army life.'

Well, well, well, thought Caroline, *our Billy is a real action man, and one with principles at that.*

When they arrived at Caroline's house, Fred accepted the offer of a cup of coffee, and as they entered, he had a good look round the hall and then the kitchen. 'Cor! This is a very nice pad, Miss Dalglish.'

'Mrs.'

'Oh sorry—Mrs Dalglish.'

When he'd gone, Caroline sat down to think about the events of the day, which had really been very interesting with exciting possibilities. In the circumstances, it seemed as though, whether she liked it or not, she was going to be involved with Billy Grant.

When Caroline woke up the next morning, she was at an emotional low. It was the first time for some weeks that she had woken with a feeling of doom. She didn't know why this should suddenly happen again after all these weeks. Most mornings had been like that for the first eighteen months after John's death. It had not just been the awfulness of his death, but also a deep feeling of guilt because she had realised, after a few months of marriage, that she was not really totally happy with him, or for that matter, in love with him. When she married him, after working for him for eighteen months, she thought she was. He was so intelligent, kind and generous, but she realised, after a while, that that was enough for a wonderful friendship, but not for marriage.

Everyone held him in such high academic esteem that when she went to work for him, helping him produce a book on medieval France, they all thought her extremely lucky, and she was. She'd been amazed that he'd selected her from all the applicants he'd had to choose from. After all, she'd only just obtained her history degree, at St Edmund Hall, and most of the others had much better qualifications. She'd worked for him for well over a year when he asked her to marry him and, at that time, he told her that he'd originally given her the job partly because he'd fallen in love with her the first time he saw her. That should really have warned her that if he could be around her, and in love with her for over a year, and not say a word or make a move, then there had to be something wrong somewhere. When they were first married, she wondered if perhaps she'd expected too much; after all, this was the first man she'd lived with or even been to bed with, perhaps books and plays over-exaggerated the physical side of a relationship. There hadn't even been anyone she could discuss it with. Her parents were both old-fashioned schoolteachers and would have been horrified by any such conversation. She'd lost touch with all her old Teddy Hall friends who might have been able to advise her. It wasn't that John didn't do romantic things, candle-lit dinners in dimly lit restaurants, a single rose in a vase beside her bed and gifts of lingerie, and he was always extremely kind and generous, but he was inept as far as physical love went. It had even been a week or so before he had managed to consummate their marriage. It had got to the stage where she actually ached with desire for some positive physical action. Then, suddenly, without warning, he was dead, and she felt awful, and guilty that she'd criticised him, even though it was only to herself, when he'd always been so good and considerate to her. She also felt slightly embarrassed to be living in the lovely, beautifully furnished house he'd left her; not that he had any other near relations. Some of his old Oxford friends, she felt sure, disapproved, not that that worried her unduly.

This combination of guilt and sorrow had made her turn in on herself; she'd lost touch with friends and had just spent all her time on turning herself into a very successful features writer. Since that time, she'd not looked at a man as anything other than possible material for her writing, and was certainly not physically attracted by any of them.

Then the affair of the Arab embassy and that horrid, chauvinistic Billy Grant. Caroline had to admit to herself that for some strange reason, being handled by that despicable man had, in some way, brought her back to life. Even thinking about his hands moving over her body made her tummy muscles tauten and gave her a strange longing in her mind and body. Urgh! How could she be so stupid?

The phone started to ring, Caroline looked at her bedside clock, it was only ten past eight—*who on earth could that be?*

Lifting the phone, she tentatively said, 'Hello, who's that?'

'Good morning, Caroline, it's Billy.'

Oh my God, she thought, *Billy Grant, and what's all this "Caroline"?* Although she knew it was childish, she couldn't resist saying, 'Billy, Billy who?'

'Billy Grant, of course, who else on such a bright, lovely morning? I didn't wake you, did I? I hope not, I had you down as an early riser.'

'No, of course not, I'm just having breakfast.' As soon as she'd said it, Caroline wondered why on earth she'd not wanted him to know that she was still lying in bed.

'Good. Can I come and see you? I want to tell you a bit more about this San Francisco business before you have your next meeting with Alastair.'

Caroline didn't want to see him, she didn't like him, and in any case, what more could there be to tell her at the moment? 'Yes,' she said. 'When do you want to meet?'

'How are you fixed today?'

'I'm busy today, I'm just finishing an article for *Cosmo*, with a deadline of tomorrow.'

'Will you be finished it by this evening? ... Yes, well great, let's make it dinner.'

'Where shall we meet?'

'I'll pick you up at your place at seven-thirty. Look forward to seeing you then.'

Caroline stretched in bed, and decided she must have gone a bit soft in the head. Billy Grant was the last person on earth she wanted to spend the evening with—well, anyway, almost the last. What on earth was she going to wear? All her clothes were good but old. John had always insisted on her having the best but, apart from a few pairs of pants, she didn't remember buying anything since he'd died. She just hadn't been interested. Here she was, a very well-paid features writer, with a private income as well, and a large valuable house filled with antiques, and all she ever spent money on was household necessities, and the occasional cheque to her parents.

Her parents; that reminded her, she must ring them, it

was ages since she'd been down to Boscastle to see them. Still, they were very happy, probably happier than ever before, now that they were retired from teaching and living in their Cornish cottage.

Their small pension seemed to cover their needs and she was able to help them with an occasional cheque, without making them feel embarrassed.

Caroline sat up in bed, she knew what was going to do today. She'd lied to Billy, she had already finished the work for *Cosmo*, and all that remained was to post the MS to them, so the day was free. She felt excited. She hadn't felt like this for ages. Her spirits, so low when she woke, were now soaring. She was going to spend the day looking round the shops and having lunch. She was out of bed in a trice, into the bathroom, showered and dress; she even hummed a little tune. As she had coffee and toast, she wondered about her hair. She got up and looked in a mirror; yes, she ought to get something done, not for Billy Grant, of course, just because it needed a bit of attention!

Although it was September, the weather was perfect, a clear blue sky, sunshine and a nice warm temperature. Caroline, having managed to get a hair appointment for eleven at Mahogany Hair Designs, decided to walk there, posting her story to *Cosmo* on the way.

Her hair was finished by twelve fifteen, and after spending a bit of time looking in the Little Clarendon Street shops, she wandered along to Browns for lunch. Whilst she was having lunch, she noticed that several men diners at other tables were obviously watching her and trying to catch her eye. She thought, *I must either be looking better again or else I've started to notice again.* Whichever it was, she felt pleased.

She was back in her house again by two fifteen and just didn't feel like doing any work. *Oh dear!* She laughed to herself, *I'm getting awful.* She made herself listen to her answerphone just in case there was an important message for her. There were two messages: one was asking her if she would interview the actor Kevin Kline for a major Sunday paper, and the second message was from her *daily*, saying she was not well, and would not be coming for a few days.

Caroline immediately phoned the Sunday to find out when they wanted the feature by. Luckily, there was no rush, and when she explained she'd be tied up for a week or so, the editor said, 'No problem, get in touch when you're free.'

Amazing, this must be her lucky day. Caroline went down to the kitchen and made herself a cup of tea, which she took back up to her first floor study. She never felt nervous in the house, although it was quite large, having on the first floor her bedroom, which was very big, an adjoining bathroom, and another large room that was a joint study and sitting room. This was where she and John had worked together on his book. On the floor above were three more double bedrooms and a bathroom. On the ground floor was a rather grand and very large drawing room, a smallish dining room, cloakroom, kitchen and a utility room. No garden at the front but a pleasant walled one at the back, where she liked to sit in the sun when she got the chance.

Caroline knew that sometime she must move, but she'd not been able to bring herself to do it just yet. She loved the house, and after all, even though it was much too big, she was able to afford to run it. For the last two years, it had, in any case, been her only extravagance. She'd be sorry to leave, and it would finally be the end of everything to do with John. She realised that the more time that passed since his death, the less she remembered that she'd not been entirely happy, and perhaps that was why she was at last beginning to get on with life again.

At six, she went to her bedroom to see what she was going to wear, after all, it wasn't every day that she went out to dinner with a man, so she might as well dress up a bit, even if it was only for horrid Billy Grant. She knew exactly what she was going to wear underneath, a ravishing lace bra with a cropped top, in a fashion colour called madeira and with it, matching lace briefs. Looking through her wardrobe, she thought again that, although all her clothes were good, a lot of them were getting rather old. She really must go up to London and have a day's shopping. As it was a lovely evening, she decided to wear a Calvin Klein ivory linen jacket, which had a fairly low-cut, scooped neckline, and with it, a short, matching, washed-silk skirt.

After her bath, Caroline massaged her body with L'Air du Temps body cream and, looking in the mirror, decided that they had made a good job of her hair. She stood back and surveyed herself. *Nothing wrong there,* she thought as she looked at the reflection of her five foot six tanned body with its long, shapely legs surmounted by a small triangle of golden fuzz, slim hips, slim waist, and well-proportioned breasts with dark, protruding nipples.

Some Mascara Parfait to accentuate the clear brilliance of her eyes, a touch of Givenchy on her cheeks and Lancome's Pastel Orange Blusher on her lips and she was ready to dress.

Before she went down to the drawing room, she looked

in the mirror and was happy with her ensemble; with the Calvin Klein suit she was wearing shear, colourless tights and navy blue, high-heeled, leather slingbacks and was carrying a matching envelope bag. She said out loud, 'Even if I say it myself, Caroline, you don't look too bad.' She giggled like a schoolgirl as she went downstairs.

At precisely seven-thirty the doorbell rang and there on the doorstep was Billy. He bowed to her then took a good look at her. 'Caroline, there is only one word that describes how you look, divine.'

Caroline was sure she was blushing, but she couldn't be, she hadn't blushed for years. It must be the embarrassment of a compliment from someone that she found so horrid. 'Thank you,' she said with difficulty, as her mouth felt all taut. 'Will you come in?'

'I'd love to, there's no rush. I've booked a table for about eight-thirty.'

'Can I offer you a drink?'

'Yes, lovely, Scotch and water please, if that's possible?'

'Help yourself to the Scotch and I'll just go and get some water.'

'Right, can I fix you something?'

'Yes, a gin and tonic please. There's some ice in the ice bucket.'

Caroline went out to the kitchen, closed the door and stood with her back against it. This was ridiculous. She felt quite weak and trembly. Surely she couldn't hate him so much that he had a physical effect on her? It must be that every time she looked at him she couldn't help remembering the horror of his long, warm hands moving over her body. She made herself move away from the door to fill a small water jug and then carry it back to the drawing room, and Billy. When she went in, he was standing by the window looking out into the Crescent, and Caroline couldn't help thinking again what a very good-looking man he was. This evening he was wearing a double-breasted, light grey, flannel suit, and it seemed to make him appear more tanned and athletic than ever. He turned as she came in and took the water jug from her.

'Here's your gin, where are you going to sit?'

Caroline didn't like it, he already had the appearance of being at home. In fact, he almost gave the impression of ownership, and he'd only been here five minutes.

'I must say,' he continued, 'I've always liked this part of Oxford. It's got something special about it. You're very lucky to have a house here, and such a nice house too.'

What did he mean? Was he trying to get at her because

she inherited all this after only being married for such a short time?

'Yes, John and I were very happy here.'

'Yes, I can imagine. It's the sort of house I could be happy in.'

Well, thought Caroline, *that may be what you think, but you'll never be here long enough to find out.* 'I guess you live in London?'

'Yes, we've a family house in Belgrave Square which I use. My father and stepmother come to London for the odd night, but otherwise I have it to myself. It's very convenient, but I prefer to be in the country if I can. What about you, are you a town or country girl?'

'I prefer the country, but Oxford suits me in my present circumstances.'

'Do you do most of your work here?'

'Yes, most of my actual writing, but I'm involved in quite a bit of field work. How's your drink? Would you like another?'

'No thanks, in any case, I suppose we'd better think about going for a spot of dinner. I've booked at the Randolph, rather unimaginative of me, but I thought if you'd been working all day you wouldn't want to travel too far.'

'No, that's fine. I hardly ever go there these days, although, John and I used to dine there quite a bit.'

Outside the house was Billy's Porsche 928s which got them to the hotel in a matter of minutes. Caroline noticed the "Car park full" notice outside the hotel garage, but Billy took no notice and drove straight in. Billy spoke to the belligerent-looking garage attendant, who immediately changed his tune and became most welcoming.

Everyone seemed to know Billy and to be pleased to see him again, even Roy, the head porter, bowed to him and said, 'How nice to see you again, Mr Grant.'

The head waiter gave them a choice of tables and they chose one in the window overlooking Beaumont Street and the Ashmolean Museum. They both decided to start with smoked salmon and to follow with Aylesbury duckling. Billy chose what Caroline knew to be a very expensive wine, Chateaux Lafite-Rothschild. Was he trying to impress her, dull her mind, or was it just the way he always lived? She had a distinct feeling it was the latter.

He smiled at her and said, 'Tell me something about yourself; all I know at the moment is that you're a devastatingly attractive widow with a very high rating as a features writer.'

'Not much to tell really. I was brought up in Thame, where my father was a master at Lord Williams's School, and where I was educated. Then I went on to St Edmund Hall, here in Oxford, where I took a history degree. You know the rest.'

'Is your father still teaching? I suppose he's Headmaster or something?'

'No, he's retired, and my parents live down in Cornwall, but he was never Head, he taught French. They say he's so good you couldn't tell him from a Frenchman.'

Caroline was beginning to warm towards Billy, and to think that perhaps he wasn't so arrogant after all, when he said, 'My word, you have done well, small town schoolteacher's daughter, and you've ended up with all this.'

'My father may have been just a small time schoolteacher, but he's more intelligent, sincere and honest than most people I know.' Her voice had an angry edge to it.

'Hey, hold on, I didn't mean that as an insult to your father, but as a compliment to you.'

'Well, I can only say you have a funny way of putting things.'

Their conversation was interrupted by the waiters serving the duckling and bringing vegetables. By the time that was done, their little disagreement was, if not forgotten, past.

'You must have a lot of men friends, Caroline, being so attractive and intelligent. Anyone special?'

'No, I don't have any, special or otherwise.'

'Good heavens, I find that hard to believe. You must be fighting them off all the time.'

'I'm really too busy to think about it.'

'But don't you miss the companionship? I can understand you not wanting to re-marry yet, but I can't see a woman like you without a relationship with a man.'

'Why should I, in particular, require a man?'

'I think most women need a man as most men need a woman. If I refer to you in particular it's because you appear to me to be, under that veneer, a warm, affectionate and probably passionate woman.'

'I really don't know how you think you've been able to deduce all that when we hardly know each other. I suppose it's because you consider that having, as I'm told, a regular harem, you're an expert on women.'

'Well, I don't know who told you that, but it's quite untrue. I may have had a few girlfriends in my time, but a regular harem, that's nonsense.'

Caroline couldn't resist saying, 'I'm very surprised,

Billy, that someone of your age and position isn't already married with a family.'

He smiled at her, and she decided that his hazel eyes were very beguiling, and said, 'There's nothing I'd like better than to give up my somewhat raffish life and to settle down with a nice, compatible woman, and to have a home and children with her. It's my dream, and incidentally, what my father wants for me as well, and is the only reason I date all these girls in the hope of finding the right one.'

My God, thought Caroline, *I'll have to watch this one with all his blarney, but I think I've got his number.*

'Oh, I do feel so sorry for you. I can see your dilemma,' she said, smiling ever so sweetly at him.

The head waiter was back, 'What would you like to follow?'

Fresh fruit salad for Caroline and ice cream for Billy. After they'd finished their sweets and were drinking their coffee, Caroline said, 'I believe you had something rather important to say to me, Billy.'

'Important to say to you?'

'Yes, that's why you said you wanted to come down this evening; to do with San Francisco?'

'Of course, the San Francisco caper. I was waiting until coffee before I broached the subject.'

Caroline, looking at him, had the distinct impression that he'd forgotten all about this "very important" discussion they were meant to have. Had he really come down just because he wanted to see her again? God forbid.

'Well,' said Billy, clearing his throat, 'I wanted to make quite sure that you understood that this is not just a straightforward piece of reporting. I don't know the full implications myself yet, but it could easily be something to do with drugs. If this guru and his sect are in some way connected with drug trafficking, then we could have a very dangerous situation on our hands. I don't want you to go into this with your eyes shut, unaware of the dangers. I must admit I'd be much happier if you told Alastair that you've decided to withdraw from this assignment. No one would think any the worse of you for it, and I for one, would be well pleased.'

Caroline had to admit that Billy really did seem sincere, but she still had the feeling that he was here more because he'd wanted to see her again than to warn her of the dangers; after all, he'd already said most of this in Sir Alastair's office. Was he after her, did he want to add her to his harem? Some chance.

'It's very kind of you to go to all this trouble to warn me, but I think I'd already got the general drift from our last meeting. I still think I'll go ahead, although it's obviously not a journalist's job. I find the whole thing rather intriguing and exciting. The last couple of years have been truly melancholic for me, so a bit of excitement, now and then, is good for me.'

'That's fine, but mind you don't bite off more than you can chew. I know you stood up well during that flap at the embassy, but I can assure you that that is nothing to what might happen if things go wrong in San Francisco.'

So, he had mentioned the embassy affair, but still no word of apology for practically stripping her and feeling her body all over. Caroline decided she could only conclude that he wasn't in the slightest sorry for what he'd done. She doubted if he even appreciated how abominable he'd behaved; he just considered, in his usual arrogant way, that whatever he did was beyond criticism.

'Well, what about you?' she asked. 'If you're going as my minder, won't you be in the same danger?'

'Maybe, and maybe not. Obviously, I'm not going to be actually with you, or the deception won't work. I've got to be very much in the background. When you're with, whoever they are, I won't be beside you. I'll be keeping an eye on your from afar. This is the main reason why I think there's too much risk for you. I just can't guarantee your safety. There's also the unexpected which one just can't plan for.'

'You're doing a pretty good job of putting me off, but I'm determined to go ahead.'

'Well, that's your decision. More coffee and brandy?'

'No thanks. That was a delicious meal.'

'I'm glad you enjoyed it. It's getting quite late. Had we better be on our way?'

As they walked through the restaurant and hotel foyer, Caroline noticed people were looking at them and realised that they must make quite a striking couple. When they went down the steps, on their way to the garage, Billy took her hand and continued to hold it until they reached his car. It gave Caroline a nice warm feeling until she reminded herself how horrid Billy was.

Arriving back at her house, Caroline asked, 'Do you want to come in for a nightcap?' And to her surprise, he accepted.

When they were seated in the drawing room, with a Scotch each, Billy said, 'Do you know Scotland well?'

'No, I don't. In fact, I've never been there.'

'Good heavens, we must do something about that. That's where my home is and I get up there as often as I can. We've got a place with a bit of land near Inverness.

It's beautiful country, if a bit rugged. Do you like walking, sailing or any of those outdoor pursuits, or are you only interested in intellectual things?'

'I don't know why you've got me marked down as some sort of wimpy member of the intelligentsia. I used to be very much an outdoor girl. I've done a lot of walking, including some in the Himalayas, swimming, surfboard sailing, team games at school and I even, believe it or not, used to follow the Beagles. So, I'm not,' she continued defensively, 'the piece of Delicate Dresden you seem to think I am.'

Billy seemed to think that very funny. He laughed away, and then said, 'I can assure you that in no way did I think of you as anything approaching wimpy. I just think of you as someone extremely beautiful who needs taking care of and cosseting.'

'That may be as it is, but you didn't give that impression in the embassy.' *Oh Lord!* she thought. *I didn't mean to say that.*

Billy looked hard at her for a minute, then said, 'Caroline, I know you hold that against me and don't seem to want to forget that unfortunate occurrence, and I even get the impression that you are not prepared to like me, or to give me a chance, because of it. I think you are being very unfair as at that time I'd not the faintest idea of who you were, and I, and my boys, were trying to sort out a difficult, and possibly dangerous, situation. Although I would like to, I can't apologise for what I did as, in the circumstances, it was the correct thing to do. I do hope that you can forgive and forget, as I'm hoping that we can become, at the very least, good friends as you're the most attractive and interesting woman I've met for a long time.'

Caroline sat back in her chair and absorbed what he'd said, she had a sneaking feeling that it made good sense. He was so handsome, confident and purposeful that she felt her heart weakening towards him. *This won't do,* she thought, *it's too early to know, perhaps he's just stringing me along.* She smiled at Billy. 'There may be something in what you say, but I'm not certain yet, after all, I hardly know you.'

'That's right, I keep forgetting that we've literally only just met. It's important, because of San Francisco, that we find out if we can get on well together, as it will be essential there. What I would like to suggest is that we spend the weekend together ... No, no, not like that, I mean at my home. It's time I went to Scotland to see my father and stepma, so I suggest you come too. It'll give us a chance to get to know each other a bit better, and we should have a bit of fun as well. I'm sure you'll like my parentals and I know they'll love you. If, at the end of the weekend, you're still not sure about me, I'll arrange for one of my other top guys to go with you instead of me. How does that sound?'

'Crikey! Which weekend do you mean?'

'This coming one, going up on Friday and coming back Monday morning.'

'Phew, that's a bit sudden,' said Caroline, thinking, *what on earth am I going to wear?* 'Yes, I suppose I could. How do we get there?'

'That's okay. I've got a company plane. I'll fly us straight to the house.'

Ask a silly question, thought Caroline, *of course he'd have a plane—doesn't everyone?* 'Yes, well, thank you very much, I accept.'

'Great, I'll phone you tomorrow evening to confirm times. If I fly to Oxford Airport, can you get there to meet me? ... Yes, good. I'll try and arrange it so that I can touch down at about ten, get you on board, and take straight off again. Anyway, I'll confirm it all when I phone.'

'What sort of clothes should I bring?'

'We're very casual up there but put in something black and slinky in case we have people in or go out to dinner one evening. Well, I suppose, regretfully I'd better head back to London.'

They went out to the front door, which Caroline opened and stood beside, and suddenly she was in his arms and their lips met in what she could only describe as a delicious, sensual kiss. Her lips seemed to melt into his, and she felt his tongue caress hers. She made herself push him gently away. She wasn't ready, or sure, that she wanted anything more.

His warm hazel eyes smiled down at her and he murmured, 'Gosh, you taste so nice I don't want to go.'

'Thank you for a lovely evening, and I'll wait to hear from you.'

She stood and waved as he drove off, then closing the door, rested her forehead against it. It had been hard to send him away. At the last minute, she'd desperately wanted him to make love to her. She stood there for some time with her head throbbing, and her body warm and moist.

CHAPTER THREE

t was only nine thirty in the morning, but Caroline's train was just arriving in London. She had woken very early and decided, on the spur of the moment, to go into London to buy some new clothes. As the train pulled alongside the platform, she told herself, once again, that it was purely because she needed a few things and not because she wanted to create a good impression at Billy's home.

Where should she start? Louis Feraud in New Bond Street? Yes, then she could work her way along Bond Street and go down into Knightsbridge if necessary. She took a taxi—this was a no-expense-spared expedition.

She enjoyed herself at Louis Feraud's Salon, she tried

lots of different, wonderful outfits, and was generally pampered; then she was shown a two-piece which she immediately fell in love with. It was in a heavenly midnight blue and made of a mohair-and-silk mixture. The jacket had well-padded shoulders, larger than Caroline was used to, and it was cut so that the front edges of the jacket did not meet but were some five or six inches apart, and fell straight to the waist and then curved away gently over the hips. The edges of the jacket were trimmed with a heavy silk ribbon, in a very subtle shade of purplish-blue. The cuffs also were trimmed with the same ribbon, and there was a long-sleeved, round-necked silk top to wear under the jacket. The straight skirt was fairly short, with longish slits, front and rear, which were lined with the same coloured silk. When Caroline looked in the mirror she knew it truly suited her and she did not need the assistant to tell her how good she looked. The cut was so clever that it even made her near-perfect figure look better. She had to have it. She asked the price. She still had to have it, although it cost more than she'd meant to spend on the entire shopping spree. By twelve, she was exhausted, but very happy with her purchases, even though she'd spent a small fortune. She had bought the beautiful Louis Feraud two-piece, for lunch or drinks parties; a

Ralph Lauren velvet shift dress with a décolleté neckline and low-scooped arm holes—the assistants went into raptures when Caroline tried this one on and said it was very sexy looking—this would do for that dinner party; and an Episode, smart but baggy, silk double-breasted jacket in dusty pink with matching pleated trousers, she could lounge around in this. Everything fitted except the trousers, they needed the bottoms finishing, but they'd be ready by mid-afternoon, so she could leave all her parcels at Episode and collect everything during the afternoon. She'd have to have lunch, but she didn't want to have it on her own, who could she ask to join her? Surprise, surprise, she thought of Billy Grant. She laughed to herself, *why not?* It would save him having to phone her this evening and would repay for last night. She asked if she could use a shop phone and dialled Billy's office number.

When she was put through, he said in a warm voice, 'Hello, Caroline, what can I do for you?'

'I'm unexpectedly in town so I wondered if you'd like to lunch with me, and then you can give me the details for tomorrow, which will save you phoning this evening.'

'I'd love to take you to lunch, where are you?'

'No, I said have lunch with me.'

'Right, thank you very much. Where shall I meet you?'

'Do you know Sheekey's, the seafood restaurant? ... At about one. See you then.'

Caroline put the receiver down and asked herself why on earth she'd done that. She didn't really want to see him, did she? What was he going to think? It made it look as if she was after him, which was exactly the opposite to the truth. Oh well, nothing she could do about it now, and anyway, she wanted to go to Sheekey's to see how it affected her. It had been one of John's favourites, and they had been there many times together. It had been what you might call *their* restaurant, and Caroline hadn't been there since his death.

She had a job to get a taxi, but even so, managed to arrive a couple of minutes before one. When she walked in the head waiter looked at her for a second and then smiling said, 'Good afternoon, Mrs Dalglish, how nice to see you, your usual table, and is Mr Dalglish with you?'

'No, a different table please and I'm afraid to say my husband died two years ago.'

'Oh, madam, I'm so very, very sorry. Are you lunching alone?'

'No, I've a friend joining me.'

At that moment Billy appeared, and holding Caroline lightly, kissed her on the cheek.

The head waiter bowed. 'Good afternoon, Mr Grant, how are you, sir?'

Oh my God! thought Caroline, *isn't there anyone that doesn't know him?*

They were still standing in the small entrance bar, and just to show who was host and in charge, Caroline asked, 'Would you like a drink here before we go to our table, or shall we go straight in?'

'Let's go to our table.'

When they were seated, they decided to have a glass of champagne as an aperitif. As she sipped hers, Caroline looked around the room. It was the same as ever with a distinct Edwardian flavour, and the walls were still covered by hundreds of signed photographs of actors, actresses and other celebrities. For a moment she thought she'd made a mistake coming here. She distinctly felt John's presence and a lump formed in her throat, and tears began to well in her eyes. Then Billy interrupted her thoughts as he gave Caroline a big smile, saying, 'This is the nicest surprise I've had for ages,' then looking at her more closely, 'are you all right, you don't look too good?'

'It's only that this was John's and my special restaurant. It's the first time I've been here since he died, and I suddenly missed him, and felt terribly sad about him.'

Billy leant across the table and took her hand. 'Caroline, I'm so sorry, perhaps we shouldn't have come here today.'

She looked into his eyes, which showed real concern, and thought that perhaps she'd been unfair to him—maybe he did have a soul after all.

'I'm sorry, Billy, it's silly of me. I'm better now. I had to come here sometime, and I think it's better that the first time it should be with someone who has nothing to do with my past life.'

'Well, as long as you're sure. Otherwise we can just up stumps, and go somewhere else.'

'No, that's sweet of you, but I'm fine now.'

He continued to look at her for a few seconds with a concerned expression, then he smiled. 'I was surprised to hear you were in town, you not having mentioned anything last night. You didn't have to come in to see Alastair, did you?'

'No, I came in on other business, and to do a bit of shopping. I haven't heard a squeak from Sir Alastair since we were there. He'd said it would be a few days anyway. Have you heard any more?'

'No, and I don't particularly want to. I did enjoy yesterday evening. I didn't want it to end when it did. Do you find me less offensive than you did before?'

'I certainly never found you that, but I must admit, I'm on the defensive when I'm with you, and I find you a bit overpowering and frightening.'

'That's very honest of you to tell me, and I'm just sorry that when we first met we got off on the wrong foot, for reasons that were beyond our control. I'm hoping that once you get to know me a bit better, you'll appreciate that I'm actually quite a quiet guy who doesn't generally go around frisking young ladies.'

They laughed together and Caroline said, 'I'm sure you don't and, as you say, it was just unfortunate the way we met. On the other hand, you probably wouldn't even have noticed me if we'd met in a more normal way.'

'Come on, I'd have noticed you however we met. You're much too beautiful to be overlooked by me, or anybody else, for that matter. After the embassy I did think about contacting you, but you seemed so angry, and to dislike me so much that I decided it was better not to. So, I'm eternally grateful to Alastair for putting me in touch with you again, especially as you've turned out to be the delightful person I was sure you must be.'

Is he sincere, or is he just scalp-hunting? Caroline couldn't make up her mind as she looked across the table at this, for her money, very attractive man. 'You do say the nicest things, Billy, but then with this "harem" of yours, I suppose you get plenty of practice on how to flatter a woman, and make her feel good?'

'I told you last night that that harem comment is just not true. The odd girlfriend or two maybe, but after all, I'm a bachelor, aren't I?'

It was like a cue in a play. Caroline couldn't help giggling about it afterwards, as at that moment in swept two fantastic-looking girls. One was wearing a shirt in vivid broken stripes, by Balmain, Caroline decided, the shortest of short white skirts, and blue-and-white high-heeled brogue courts. The other was in a very short white shift, with a low-cut, scooped neckline and with it an Op Art chiffon over-layer; white high-heeled slingbacks completed her ensemble. Caroline doubted whether either of them was wearing much else, well, brief briefs maybe, and certainly perfume! On the way to their table, they suddenly spotted Billy and with shrieks they descended on him. As he tried to stand up, they both hugged and kissed him as if he was the last man on Earth. They almost ignored Caroline when Billy tried to introduce them, and asked if they could join his table.

'No,' he said, 'not possible.'

They were so scintillating, so full of fun, so obviously naughty, and enjoying life to its fullest that Caroline began to wonder if she was really rather staid, and too set in her ways. Until they'd arrived, she'd felt that in her sugar-pink, wool hipster with its black braiding and buttons, and straight black wool skirt, she was the most adventurously, and stylishly dressed woman in the restaurant. But now, with these two girls beside her flashing their long legs, and everything else they'd got, she felt positively frumpish. After what was a few minutes, but seemed an age to Caroline, with more hugging and kissing, off they went to their own table.

'Well, well, Billy, those are what I'd describe as the perfect sort of friends for a nice quiet guy who doesn't know many girls, and certainly doesn't like *harems*.'

Affecting a hang-dog look, and looking at her from under his brows, as she began to laugh, he muttered, 'I don't really know them all that well.' And then he began to laugh as well.

It was a very good lunch, the food was just right as it had always been at Sheekey's, and Caroline and Billy seemed to have reached a new stage of their friendship. Caroline wasn't necessarily more certain of his intentions, if he had any, but she felt better prepared to deal with him. He was a very powerful man, both physically and mentally, self-assured, confident and determined to get what he wanted, but she was not so sure that he was as ruthless as she'd first thought. It was, she realised, that suspected ruthlessness that had put her off and frightened her.

'As I'm now going to be away with you in Scotland, do you think I ought to let Sir Alastair know, in case he tries to contact me?'

'We could pop around there now, if you like, and see if we can have a word with him.'

'It might be a good idea.'

'Let's have a drop more coffee then, by which time Fred will have arrived to pick me up.'

'Tell me, Billy, what is Sir Alastair really? He told me he's a government press liaison officer, but that's obviously nonsense.'

Billy laughed. 'He's a funny old bird. I don't know why he tells people these strange stories, after all, if you're going to work for him, you're going to know, sooner or later, what he's up to. He and my father met during the Hitler war, and although they've never been chums, they've kept in touch, so I've known him vaguely forever. He was a top man in MI6, and then when a reorganisation took place, he moved to MI5. He did, I'm told, a brilliant job there, but didn't want to go when he reached retiring age. When they said they couldn't let him stay he threatened that, unless they arranged something, he'd write his memoirs. This frightened everyone no end, my dad says that Alastair's been associated with so much skulduggery that he could discredit at least half the people who have ever been associated with government during the last forty years. I imagine that that's a slight exaggeration, but there was enough to make the powers-that-be think very carefully. Some mandarin came up with the bright idea, that as Alastair was not really fit to stay on with MI5, of starting a small intelligence agency for him to run. Nothing very important or large, just a small show to keep him happy. So, that's what they did, and now they give him small, non-crucial matters to handle. He's got virtually no permanent staff, so that's why he uses me and my company, and why he tries to recruit people like you, when he needs them, for field work. In the main, it's all pretty small stuff but it does mean that he can carry on within his own little clandestine world, and everyone's happy.'

'Except perhaps the poor taxpayers, if they knew.'

'Yes, I agree, but he has actually paid for himself, and must be in credit. I can't tell you the ins and outs, but about a year ago he tumbled onto someone who worked at the Communications Centre who was selling fairly crucial information to a foreign power. That alone justified his costs for many years, and in any case, it's just a drop in the ocean compared to all the other things that large amounts of money are wasted on. His success over that one does also mean that one must take seriously his other projects, like San Francisco.'

A waiter came over to their table with a message that Billy's car was waiting in St Martin's Lane. When the bill came, Billy said, 'Caroline, please let me do this.'

'No, Billy, I asked you to join me.'

'Okay, thank you very much. The food was excellent, and the quality of the company, beyond words.'

They smiled at each other as they got up to leave, and Billy took Caroline's hand, and squeezed it before standing aside for her to go out of the restaurant—his hand, instead of feeling threatening to her, as it had done, now felt warm and comforting.

As they came out of Sheekey's they could see the black Range Rover parked at the end of St Martin's Lane with the enormous, and nonchalant, figure of Fred leaning against it. As they approached him, his face puckered into a grin, making him look more like a pirate than ever.

'Hello, boss, afternoon, Mrs Dalglish, 'ave a good lunch?'

As they were moving off, Caroline explained to Billy that she'd some things to collect from Brampton Road, and that if she went to the Victoria Street office first the shop might well be closed before she could get back there.

'No problem,' he said. 'Let's ring Alastair, and see how he's placed this afternoon, and then we can decide what we're going to do.' He spoke on the car phone, and then turning to Caroline said, 'Yes, he can see us just whenever we get there. As it's now three fifteen, Fred can drop me at my office, take you wherever you want to go, and then pick me up again on the way to Alastair. What do you think?'

'I'm being much too much trouble. If you let me out here, I'll get a cab and meet you at Sir Alastair's office in about forty-five minutes.'

'Caroline, you could never be too much trouble as far as I'm concerned. That's settled then. Can you drop me at the office, Fred, and then take Mrs Dalglish to Brampton Road, and then back again to pick me up. I'd come with you, Caroline, but I have a couple of things I ought to see to, especially as we're going to Scotland tomorrow.'

Everything was ready for her at Episode, so she was

only there for a few minutes, and then she and Fred were on their way back to collect Billy. They chatted as he forced his way through the traffic. Caroline had begun to think of Fred as an old friend and had almost forgotten the embarrassing circumstances of their first meeting. Fred dialled a number on the phone and said to someone, 'Will you tell the boss that I'll be outside in about six minutes.' Caroline was very impressed with their procedures. They certainly seemed to save themselves as much hassle as possible. This was an organisation that, if Billy would agree, she could certainly do an interesting feature on. She'd have to take it up with him when this other business was finished. For the rest of the journey, she sat musing on how she would write it, and what publication she would offer the feature to.

Billy's office turned out to be a rather smart building in Queen Anne's Gate, just off Victoria Street, and only a couple of minutes from Sir Alastair Brown's headquarters. Billy came out of the door as they drew up in front of the building. Caroline thought that every time she saw him, he appeared a bit more handsome, and dashing. She'd have to watch herself. She was beginning to like him a little bit too much. He climbed in the front seat beside her, so there she was between great, big Fred and great, big Billy. Billy's thigh felt warm against hers, and she suddenly had a wild desire to rest her hand on it. She stopped herself and gave a little nervous laugh instead.

'What's funny?' asked Billy.

'Oh, er, nothing really. It's just that I thought how surprised any of my friends would be if they saw me squashed between you two he-men in this black Range Rover.'

'You're not too squashed, are you? It felt just right to me. I'll see if I can move a bit to make you more comfortable.' He moved forward a little and then brought his right arm onto the back of the seat behind her, his hand stroked her hair for a second, before he stretched his arm along the back of the seat. Now, far from being further apart, their bodies were in contact from shoulder to knee. Still, Caroline had to admit it felt rather nice. 'You all right, Fred?' he asked.

'I'm fine, boss. I'd be quite happy driving about like this all the time.'

The two men laughed heartily.

'I take it that's meant as a compliment, Fred?' Caroline asked, having caught their jocular mood.

'What else, Mrs D?'

They were now in Victoria Street and pulled up

outside Alastair Brown's office. Fred was out in a flash—he moved so quickly and effortlessly for such a massive man—and moved to the front door to give instructions for it to be opened. Billy opened his car door, and getting out, turned to assist Caroline. As she slid across the seat, she knew her short skirt was riding up—but let it—she'd show him whose legs were better, hers, or those of his two flash girlfriends from Sheekey's! Billy took her arm to help her down from the high Range Rover seat, but he didn't move back, so when her feet reached the pavement, their bodies were touching. She didn't dare raise her face as she knew instinctively that if she did, he would kiss her full on the lips, despite the fact that it was broad daylight, and that they were outside Sir Alastair's office, right in the middle of bustling Victoria Street. After a short pause, Billy moved to one side, and Caroline, with her heart fluttering, went towards the now open door of the building. She smiled at Fred as she went through the door, and heard Billy ask him to wait somewhere with the car as he would phone him when they were ready to leave.

They had to wait in reception for a few minutes before being shown up to Sir Alastair's room. As the went in, he came forward to greet them and said, 'Good afternoon, Caroline. I may call you that, may I? Good, and please call me Alastair. Hello Billy; now please sit down, and you'll have a cup of tea, won't you? Well Caroline, have you decided whether you want to help us with our little project? Good, then I think we can get onto the next stage. Ah, good, here's the tea.'

Everything stopped while the tray was set down and the tea was poured for the three of them. 'Will you have a chocolate biscuit, Caroline?' asked Alastair. Her eye caught Billy's and she couldn't hold back a smile. He grinned and winked. She thought, *It's all so incongruous. I'm having tea just as though I'm in an Oxford don's sitting room for an intellectual discussion, but actually I'm just about to discuss a clandestine operation with a "spymaster" and my "minder". What would John think of all this?* She had a horrid feeling he would thoroughly disapprove.

'What we're waiting for now is an advertisement to appear. This sect use some of the specialist publications to invite people to become involved. The advertisement gives very few details and simply asks people interested to write in. When they receive a letter from an interested party, they invite the person concerned to go and meet their UK organiser. From then on, we're not too sure what happens, but we think they'll then do a bit of checking-up. After all this, if they consider the person concerned suitable, they must invite them to visit their guru in San Francisco. We don't know whether they pay the airfares or not, or how many of the detailed arrangements are seen to by them. So, Caroline, what we're suggesting is that once an advertisement appears, and from our experience there should be one anytime now, we'll get you to respond to it. You'll use as your address one that I'll give you that is a London one used by both us and the Foreign Office. That way we can control any attempts they make to check you out. The staff there will say that you live there, etc., and will take any telephone messages that come in for you, for relaying to us, and then to you. You'll then be quite safe from any interference at your own home. When they've made contact with you, you'll need to go to whatever meeting they suggest, before we know what further arrangements they're going to suggest, and how we're going to react. Is that all clear, as far as it goes?'

'Yes, perfectly clear, thank you, Alastair.' Caroline was amazed at her own voice. It was so calm and matter-of-fact, just as though she was doing this sort of thing all the time. She wished she looked a little more the part, surely she ought to look like Marlene Dietrich, and be wearing a black dress with long slits up either side of her skirt. Was this really her sitting here listening to all these things, and perhaps getting herself into a very dangerous situation? It all sounded so absurd, that she was only just beginning to realise that it was for real, and not just a game. She looked across at Billy. Yes, he was obviously taking it all seriously.

'Now, Caroline, are you sure there's nothing you want to ask at this stage?'

She couldn't think of anything, but she thought that they'd both expect her to ask some pertinent question or questions—what on earth could she ask? 'How long do you think it will be from the time of the first contact to my setting off for San Francisco?'

'That's a very difficult question to answer. Is it important?'

'Yes, as you'll appreciate, it's very difficult for me to undertake any commissions when I don't know whether I'm going to be here or not.'

'That's a very good point, Alastair. How long can you expect Caroline to sit around waiting? After all, she's a working girl, having to earn her own living.'

'Of course, Billy, you're both right. What I'll do, Caroline is, from next Monday, have you put on half-pay as a retainer, until such time as the job either starts in earnest or is aborted. Is that fair?'

'Yes, I'd say that's very fair. Thank you, Alastair.'

Caroline couldn't resist looking at Billy, whom she found was looking at her intently.

The whole business seemed to be getting more and more ludicrous. Why on earth had she allowed herself to become involved in the first place? After all, she was very happy doing her features, and living in Oxford, wasn't she? That of course was the answer. She wasn't all that happy. It was just that she'd sunk into a rut, and what with John and everything she just hadn't realised. There was something else as well—Billy! What were her feelings about him? Her thoughts were interrupted by the sound of Alastair's voice asking a question, what on earth was he saying? 'Another cup of tea? Oh, no thank you, Alastair.'

The three of them talked on for a while, going over some of the points again, but it was decided that there was nothing else that could be done until the advertisement appeared. It was almost six when they finally left Alastair's office and went down to reception to await Fred's arrival.

'Have dinner with me.'

'No, I can't. I must get back to Oxford.'

'Do you have to go back so early?'

'Yes, I've got to pack, and get everything ready for tomorrow.'

'Can't you do it in the morning?'

'No, there wouldn't be time.'

'We could go a little later then.'

'No, Billy, let's leave the arrangements as they are.'

'I could drive you down to Oxford and we could have dinner there.'

'No, thank you. I want the evening to myself, and in any case my car is at Oxford Station.'

'Then Fred will drive you to Oxford Station.'

'I'm sure he doesn't want to do that.'

'Yes, he'll do it. Do you want to have a drink at my place first?'

'No, thank you.'

The large man in green arrived to say the car was outside. Caroline could see Billy was not very pleased that she wouldn't fall in with his plans. He was definitely a man who liked to get his own way.

As the car took him round to his office, Billy gave Caroline instructions on where to go and where to leave her car next morning at Oxford Airport.

He would land at approximately ten and take off again as quickly as possible. When they pulled up outside Billy's office building, he asked, 'Are you sure you won't change your mind about dinner?' When she said no, he kissed her on the cheek, and left without a backward glance. As Fred drove Caroline through the heavy traffic, she let her mind dwell on the day's events. It had been a real fun day, and she couldn't wait to look at the clothes she'd bought. She still hadn't made up her mind about Billy. He no longer appeared the ogre that she'd first imagined him, but he was certainly very strong-willed and, she thought, a little too arrogant. The way he fooled about when those two girls arrived at Sheekey's proved that he was still boyish at heart, and ready for some fun. What did he think about her? Was he just trying to get her into bed, or was there more to it than that? He was a very attractive man, and she had to admit that when he put his arm round her in the car, and even more when their bodies were touching as she got out of the car in Victoria Street, she had felt a flame of desire in the pit of her stomach; just as she had last night when he kissed her. Phew! She really was beginning to fancy him, but she wasn't going to let him just bed her and say goodbye, as she was sure he had to lots of other girls. That was not her style. If she had a relationship with him, she wanted it to be meaningful. She smiled to herself, how her thoughts had changed in the last couple of days. She was beginning to feel more alive than she had for ages and ages.

After Fred dropped her at Oxford Station, she drove

straight home, and really had very little time to think about Billy, or anything else, as she prepared her things for the weekend away.

CHAPTER FOUR

On Friday morning Caroline arrived at Oxford Airport with plenty of time to spare. Mr Crawford, whom she had been told to seek, turned out to be a nice little man who soon had her car parked, and took her into an office for a cup of coffee.

As they sat chatting, she asked, 'Do you know Billy Grant well?'

'I can't say I know him well, but I've seen quite a bit of him over the last year or two.'

'Does he keep his plane here sometimes?'

'No, but he used to come in and out of here a fair number of times. There were some Arab princes that were studying somewhere in the city and Mr Grant's organisation was responsible for their security, and for transporting them to various functions. I like dealing with Mr Grant. He may be tough, but he's very fair, and you know exactly where you are with him.'

They received word that Billy's plane was just about to land so Mr Crawford got Caroline and her baggage into a car to take out to the aircraft. Caroline began to feel just a little nervous; she's never been in a small private plane before.

'I expect Mr Grant's a very experienced pilot,' Caroline said, hoping for a reassuring reply.

'Oh, my word, yes, Mrs Dalglish, he's one of the best I've ever been with. One year, I'd done a few things for him, and as a thank-you he took me over to Paris for a Christmas lunch, and on the way back the weather was unbelievable. I wouldn't have wanted to be with anyone else, I can tell you. Here we are, he's taxiing over now.'

Caroline didn't know what she'd expected, a little tiny plane with one engine, just room for two inside? Instead of which, coming towards her was a sleek, twin-engined aircraft, white with red coach lines along the sides, and four or five side windows indicating that it had an executive-type cabin.

Turning to Mr Crawford, she said, 'That looks very

smart and workmanlike.'

'Good Lord, yes, Mrs Dalglish, that's a Cessna 421C Golden Eagle. A very, very nice aircraft.'

The plane came to a halt, and the engines were turned off. As they drove towards it, Billy got out and waved.

'Hello, Caroline. Good morning, Crawford, very kind of you to look after Mrs Dalglish for me.'

'My pleasure, Mr Grant, and very nice to see you again.'

Within a few minutes, the luggage was loaded, and they were ready for take-off, with Caroline sitting up front next to Billy. Billy was talking on his radio and checking switches etc. as the plane moved round and out onto the runway, where it stopped and remained motionless. He turned and laughingly said, 'Hang on, here we go.'

They were off down the runway at an ever-increasing speed, then the plane lifted and was airborne. Caroline felt a few seconds of panic, then she felt great. It was as if her spirits were lifting in tune with the plane. It was a beautiful sunny morning, and as she looked down, she could see the city of Oxford with the sun glinting on the River Thames, as it wound its way through the city, and the surrounding countryside.

As Billy was still jabbering away on the radio, she was able to concentrate on the scenery. Then she turned and had another look round the inside of the plane. Not what she'd expected—quite spacious and very luxurious with seats for eight people.

'There's some coffee in the thermos in the bar cupboard, and some biscuits and things, if you'd like to see to it, Caroline. You'll find mugs there as well. I'll have black please.'

She undid her belt and walked gingerly back down the plane. It really was rock steady, the coffee didn't even spill when she poured it. She found a small tray and took their coffee back to the cockpit.

'Thanks,' Billy said with a smile. 'Weather conditions are good, with a slight tail wind, so we should be there well in time for lunch.'

'What, at your home?'

'Yes, it's about five hundred and twenty-five miles, so we should be there before one.'

'I thought little planes were very slow, so I expected to be up here for hours and hours.'

Billy laughed. 'You would be in some of them, but this cruises at two hundred and fifty miles per hour and has a non-stop range of one thousand five hundred miles.'

She could see he loved this plane and was very proud of it.

'It must have cost and awful lot of money and be very expensive to run.'

'It did cost quite a bit, but if you take into account the convenience factor, it's not too bad to run. You must remember that I use it for transporting my boys and clients most of the time, and not for transporting beautiful young ladies. With the latter, of course, and in particular cases, it's worth every penny, and more.'

'What do you mean by "particular cases", that you get them marooned up here, and have your way with them?'

'That's a good idea, I hadn't thought of that one,' he replied, laughing. 'The only trouble is, I'm too careful a pilot to let this thing fly itself.'

'That's a relief then.'

'Why, don't you think you'd like to be made love to while floating up in the clouds?'

'I wouldn't like that to happen anywhere against my will.'

'Quite right, and anyway, one should always feel as though one is floating in the clouds when one makes love, shouldn't one?' Billy said, turning to grin at her.

He's making fun of me, she thought, so she just smiled back at him sweetly and said nothing.

Caroline thought to herself that here she was, about

to spend the weekend with Billy's parents and she knew nothing about them. She had met quite a few titled people at Oxford—academics, politicians and rewarded civil servants. She wondered what Billy's father had got his for. He'd been in the army, perhaps it was for that. Anyway, she thought she'd better know before she met him.

'Billy, what did your father get his title for?'

'For being his father's son.'

'And why did his father get his?'

'For the same reason. My father is the sixth Lord Grant.'

'Oh, I see, does that mean that one day you'll be the seventh?' asked Caroline, trying to sound as though it was the sort of question she was having to ask people all the time.

'That's right, but not for a long time yet, I hope.'

The sun was shining, and the weather perfect for flying the whole way up. Caroline really enjoyed the journey, and was almost disappointed when Billy said, 'Not long now, about twenty minutes or so.'

Looking down, she saw they were beginning to fly over what looked like a great lake.

'What's that water down there?'

'That's the famous Loch Ness, you know, where the

monster is.'

'Have you ever seen it?'

'No, I'm never that drunk!'

Billy banked the plane and they started to pass the Loch and approached, what appeared to Caroline, to be a small cluster of cottages and houses with a castle to the rear. It all looked very romantic in the September sun. She wondered which was the Grant's family home. She thought it must be the largish one she could see standing a bit apart from the others. She wondered if the castle was inhabited or if it was just a national monument. She was just about to ask Billy when he said, 'A chap called MacDonald will be at the strip to meet us. Don't worry if he seems a bit rude, that's just his way. He saved my father's life when they were in the war together, and was badly wounded, so he's been here ever since, as a sort of general factotum and honorary member of the family. He still suffers quite a bit of pain, and in any case, he doesn't much care for most people.'

Well, that's sounds like a good start, thought Caroline. *Now he'll go on to tell me about the dragons that roam about at night looking for delectable young girls to ravage and eat.* She burst out laughing, much to her surprise, and to his.

'What's funny?'

'Well, er ... nothing really. I just thought it funny that I was here, that's all.'

The conversation was dropped as the plane's wheels touched the ground. It came to a halt near a hanger, outside of which was parked a Range Rover. Billy switched everything off.

Then Caroline saw this character coming towards the plane. Having never been to Scotland before she was thrilled to have sight of her first *wild* Highlander. He was in an old, patched kilt, sporran and all, knee-length hose going down to highly polished black brogues, a wool shirt, and on his head he had a bonnet with, what Caroline thought must be, an eagle's feather stuck in it. As she was the first out of the plane, she walked up to him and, holding out her hand, said, 'You must be Mr MacDonald.'

'Aye! I am that,' he said and took her hand. He held it rather than shook it and looked into her clear blue eyes. He smiled and nodded, and from that moment on, he was hers to command.

When they had put the cases into the Range Rover, MacDonald opened the passenger door for Caroline, and helped her in. She saw Billy watching them with a surprised, pleased look.

'I'll come back and put the plane away later or we'll be late for lunch,' Billy said to MacDonald.

As they drove towards the houses, Caroline could see the very impressive castle in the background and wanted to ask about it, but Billy and MacDonald were bringing each other up to date with their news. They drove past the houses, up to the castle, through the gates, into a courtyard, and stopped.

'Here we are, Caroline, home sweet home. Not too bad a journey, was it? Under three hours all told.'

Caroline didn't answer for a minute; she was sitting there just thinking to herself, *what am I doing here? The sixth Baron, and their home a castle. These people are out of my league—out of another world.* 'I didn't know you lived in a castle, Billy, you never told me.'

'I'm sorry, I never thought of mentioning it. It doesn't matter really, does it? I can assure you it's rather comfortable and it's got all modern cons.'

She laughed. He didn't even realise what she was getting at.

MacDonald was helping her out of the Range Rover when out of the front door came a very beautiful woman. She was, in a way, like an older version of Caroline. An inch or so shorter than Caroline, she had the same perfect figure, long blonde hair, and clear, sparkling blue eyes. Although she was only wearing a navy blue, pleated skirt, with an open-necked, cream silk shirt and low-heeled, navy courts, she looked most elegant. Billy stepped forward and they gave each other a big hug and kiss. Turning, he said, 'This is Caroline; Caroline, this is my stepma, Elizabeth.'

The two women shook hands, appraised each other, and it was obvious both liked what they saw.

'Why don't you two just freshen up and do your unpacking after lunch?'

'Good idea. Which room is Caroline in?'

'We've put her in the pink room, do you think she'll like that?'

'Yes, I think that's just her. I'll get someone to help with the bags.'

'Nay bother, I'll be putting yon lassie's bags in her room,' said MacDonald.

'Oh, thanks, MacDonald,' Billy said, and he and Elizabeth looked at each other and grinned. 'Come on, Caroline, I'll show you the way.'

They went into an enormous hall with a flagstone floor, and panelled walls with claymores, swords and lances hanging from them. In one corner there was even a full suit of armour. Then up a great oaken staircase that halfway divided into two, one part going in each direction. MacDonald preceded them, with Caroline's case, down various close-carpeted corridors until he eventually opened a large oak door and stood aside for Caroline to enter. It was a beautiful room, the most beautiful bedroom Caroline had ever been in. A very feminine room with a pink-and-white colour scheme. The walls were curved as it was situated in a turret, and the narrow, latticed windows all had padded window seats. Even the carpet was basically pink-and-white, and the poster bed had pink-and-white hangings. The furniture was white French with gilt adornments, and the walls were hung with peaceful watercolours. MacDonald put her case down, and Billy opened the door to her bathroom. She thanked MacDonald for carrying her case up, then turning to Billy said. 'How on earth do I find my way to wherever we're lunching?'

'How long do you want to freshen up—ten minutes? Great, I'll come and collect you.'

When he and MacDonald had gone, she just stood for a minute looking round this large, sumptuous room. Then she went into the bathroom, it was as big as her bedroom at home. It was fitted with everything; it even had a chaise lounge!

When Billy collected her from her room, he took the opportunity to take her briefly in his arms and kiss her. 'You always smell so delicious, and look so divine, I just want to hug you to death.'

'I'd rather you took me down for some lunch, I'm starving.'

'You don't 'alf know how to put a chap in his place.' He laughed.

There were only the three of them for lunch, Lord Grant was in Inverness for the day. They chatted about all sorts of things, and Caroline was able to work out, from what she said, that Lady Grant was about forty-six years old, although she looked more like thirty-six. It was also obvious that Elizabeth Grant and Billy thought a lot of each other, and that Billy's father meant a very great deal to them both. They told her that Billy's stepbrother and stepsister were in Australia visiting cousins who had a vineyard there. Caroline could see this was a very united, happy family.

All through lunch Billy kept smiling across the table at her, and she could see that Elizabeth noticed and was amused. 'How long have you and Billy known each other?'

'You'll never believe this, we met last Tuesday. Well,

that's not absolutely correct, I did meet Billy once before, but only vaguely, on business.'

'Oh, how exciting, it's so nice making new friends. You said on business, Caroline, what do you do?'

'I'm a freelance features writer.'

'But of course, Caroline Dalglish. How stupid of me, the penny hadn't dropped. I know your name well and have read lots of your articles. I think you write extremely well. We're honoured to have such a celebrity staying with us. Why didn't you let me know, Billy? We could have had a big party and shown Caroline off, that would have made all our stuffy old friends sit up.'

Caroline looked at her, was she having her leg pulled? No, she could see Lady Grant meant what she said. It was always a shock when people like this had heard of her and were impressed by her work. 'That's very kind of you to say so, Lady Grant.'

'It's not kind of me, your work is very impressive, and please call me Elizabeth.'

'Thank you,' Caroline said, smiling at her.

Billy laughed. 'Is it really that good, Elizabeth? I've never read any of it. I thought it was just rubbishy stuff in women's mags.' He looked at Caroline and she poked her tongue out at him.

'Really, Billy, you are at times a bit of a philistine. What a rude thing to say to Caroline. I particularly remember that brilliant series you did for a Sunday colour supplement comparing the major European universities. Am I right that you even took most of the photographs yourself?'

'I do know that she's a dab hand at the odd photo. You've even been known to take them in places were they're not allowed, haven't you, Caroline?'

'You know, Elizabeth, you can go quite off a person, can't you?'

They all laughed, and Elizabeth gave the two of them a quizzical look, knowing that there was more to this than met the eye.

'Have you and Father arranged anything for the weekend?'

'Well, we didn't really know what you'd both want to do, so all we've fixed so far is a dinner party for tomorrow evening. We thought we'd open up the large dining room and have a mildly grand affair.'

What then, thought Caroline, looking round, *is this room, if it isn't an enormous dining room?*

'That sounds great, doesn't it, Caroline?'

Caroline was going to say that she hoped they weren't

going to a lot of trouble on her account, but she thought better of it, and just said, 'Yes, terrific.'

'As it's nearly three, why don't you two go up and unpack? We can have a cup of tea on the terrace at four fifteen, after which Billy can give you a tour of the castle and gardens. Alexander should be back about four-ish, so you'll be able to meet him then, Caroline.'

When they reached Caroline's bedroom, Billy opened the door, and standing against it, put his arm around her waist and pulled her to him. She looked up and their lips met in a long, lingering kiss. It felt good, it felt very good. Her legs felt weak, her head spun. He whispered in her ear, 'Darling, shall I come in and have a siesta with you?'

As she felt his hard body pressed against her, physically she wanted to say *yes*, but even though her mind was lulled by the good food, wine and romantic surroundings, she managed to maintain her resolve, and to say, 'No, Billy, I must unpack.'

He didn't let go of her immediately, but as she turned her face away so that he couldn't reach her lips, and just stood passively in his arms, he eventually, with a long sigh, let her go.

'I'll see you later then,' she said, shutting the door behind her.

As she stood by the closed door, she could hear him move away, and she realised that she was trembling slightly. Oh Lord, she wanted to be made love to, but she knew she was right not to have let her emotions run away with her. She was still not at all sure of his intentions. Was he just trying to get closer to her because of their impending job in San Francisco, or was it because he wanted to have a lasting relationship with her, or just simply that he desired her sexually? She had a strong suspicion it was the latter.

What about her feelings for him, had they changed? Yes, they certainly had. She had decided she hated him after their first meeting, but now she didn't, and she appreciated that what he did that day at the embassy he'd had to do. She still felt him to be arrogant, self-willed, self-centred and difficult. But he was awfully handsome, masculine, authoritative and desirable. She laughed out loud as she thought how much she would like to lie on this lovely big bed with him with their naked bodies entwined. *This won't do,* she thought, *I'd better get on with my unpacking.*

Just after four, there was a tap on the door and it opened with Billy calling out, 'Are you respectable?'

'Yes, come in.'

'That's a pity,' he said, laughing. 'I thought I might catch you in your smalls. You do look nice.'

Caroline had changed into an ivory slub jacket, with ebony-and-ivory-spot culottes and low-heeled ivory suede slingbacks. 'Thank you, kind sir,' she said.

When they arrived at the terrace, tea was waiting, and Lord Grant had arrived. He stood up and came forward to meet them.

'Caroline, this is my father. Father, this is my friend, Caroline Dalglish.'

It was amazing, Caroline thought as she shook hands, he was just exactly an older version of Billy. Same height, same colouring and same manner. He was a very impressive, and still attractive, man. 'How do you do?' they both said, with him smiling down at her. 'Please come and sit here beside me. Elizabeth has just been telling me that you are *the* Caroline Dalglish. We have enjoyed some of your stuff very much indeed.'

'That's extremely kind of you to say so.' Caroline was almost overwhelmed, Lord and Lady Grant were so kind, and she could tell they really meant what they said, treating her as though she was the VIP when all the time, he was undeniably a very important man, the sixth Baron, living in a castle, and certainly very rich. She noticed that even Billy was beginning to look at her with a certain amount of respect, having heard all these compliments from his parents.

'I don't know what's happened to Billy,' Lord Grant said, 'He must be maturing at last, bringing up a nice, intelligent, young lady like you, instead of one of his usual scatterbrains.' They all laughed. 'I hear you were the wife of John Dalglish, the historian. I met him a few times when I was on an Oxford appeals committee. A brilliant man, his death was a tragedy.'

'How nice that you actually met him. He was, as you say, a brilliant man. He was also the kindest, most considerate person imaginable.'

'You must miss him very much,' Elizabeth said.

'Yes, I do. It's just the last few months that I've started to get over it.'

'Come on,' said Billy, 'if you've finished your tea, I'll give you the *two-pound* tour.'

'I think you may find it amusing as you're interested in history,' said Lord Grant.

'Yes, I'm sure I will. How long have you had the castle?'

'The family moved here, when their old home was destroyed, about five hundred and sixty years ago.'

Well, thought Caroline, *there's really no answer to that.*

She and Billy excused themselves and went off round the castle. It was magnificent. A lot of the rooms—and she lost count of how many there were—were what one might call slightly shabby, but that somehow added to, rather than distracted from, the general feeling of richness. It took quite a time to get round, Billy knew every inch, and plainly loved the place. They ended up in the Great Hall. 'This,' said Billy, 'is where we'll have dinner tomorrow evening.'

Caroline, looking round it, could see why earlier Elizabeth had referred to the *large* dining room. It was a huge room, going right up to the rafters, and having an enormous inglenook fireplace at each end. The walls were adorned with more ancient weapons, armour and stags' heads.

When they'd finished inside, they went out into the gardens, which were landscaped, having rose terraces, lavender walks, lawns and even a small lake.

'Caroline, I'm sure I've tired you out, and as it's already gone half-six, perhaps you'd like to go and have a bath and change. It's nothing grand tonight, just the four of us. We'll meet for a drink at about seven-thirty.'

Billy escorted her back to her room, and said, 'I'll come and collect you at about half-seven.'

When she was lying in a hot, perfumed bath she relaxed and thought about her amazing day that must seem mundane to the Grant family. Flying up to Scotland in that super plane, meeting Lord and Lady Grant who lived in a home their family had been in for, what was it, five or six hundred years? They were so charming and welcoming, but they must be thinking, *What's Billy doing with this little nobody?* It was a mistake to have come. In the circumstances, Billy could be after only one thing, and although she was now very physically attracted to him, she decided she was not going to sleep with him. If she did, it would almost be as if he were paying for it. It would make her feel like a cheap tart. It would, she mused, almost certainly be very enjoyable, but she just couldn't do it. He hadn't even respected her for her work until his parents made something of it. He must just think of her as something he could have a bit of fun with for a few nights. He was so jolly attractive that she could understand he could get almost any girl he wanted, *but not this one*, she decided, somewhat mournfully.

After her bath, she did her hair and make-up carefully. She wanted to look nice for Lord and Lady Grant. The dress she'd brought with her for this evening was one of her old favourites, a short Mark Jacobs silver pave slip. It left her shoulders and arms bare, except for two narrow silver shoulder straps. It was too low-cut to wear a bra, so all she wore with it were briefs, shear tights and high-heeled silver slingbacks. Looking in the mirror, she was pleased with her reflection. Not bad for a nearly middle-aged—twenty-five must be nearly middle-aged—little widow nobody. She couldn't help giggling to herself.

When Billy came to collect her, he just stood and stared for a minute. 'You're the most gorgeous thing I've ever seen, I just can't believe it. I've got to touch you to see if you're real.' With that he put his arm round her waist and kissed her on the lips. He stepped back. 'My God! Yes, you're certainly flesh and blood, no mistaking that.'

They went downstairs together and into the sitting room for a drink before dinner.

Over dinner they all got on very well, talked about a variety of subjects and laughed a lot. Caroline could tell that Billy was surprised that she could discuss so many subjects in a knowledgeable manner. She thought, *He really is a bit of a chauvinist,* just as she'd thought when they'd first met.

Elizabeth suggested coffee in the sitting room. When they were sitting down, and coffee had been brought by one of the girls who helped in the house, Lord Grant turned to Caroline and asked, 'Have you always lived in Oxford?'

'No, I was brought up in a small nearby town, called Thame.'

'Her father was a teacher at the local school,' Billy interposed. He didn't say it sneeringly or anything like that, but there was a slightly patronising edge to his voice that Caroline didn't like. It was as though he was indicating that her father had never done anything that was not mundane and ordinary. It hurt her, there was nothing she could say. It was probably true, but she loved her father, and he was so intelligent and dependable. Just because Billy only liked people that were positive and dynamic, didn't give him the right to be critical about all the rest. She was glad she had decided not to sleep with him.

'Not Lord Williams's School?' asked Lord Grant.

'Yes, do you know it?'

'I used to go there to see someone I served with for a short time in 1940; a man called George Johnson.'

'That's my father.'

They all exclaimed what an extraordinary coincidence it was as, of course, none of them had known Caroline's maiden name.

'How did you meet him, Lord Grant? I know he served

in something or other, but I've never been too sure quite what.'

'You mean you didn't know that your father was a war hero? No, well I'm damned! He's a first-class linguist, as I'm sure you must know, and he spent the war working with the French Resistance in France. What he did makes your little old SAS lot look pretty tame, Billy. He was a legend. At the end of the war, he not only got a Croix de Guerre, but also from General De Gaulle personally, the Legion of Honour. I was down seeing him because some of us, who considered him one of the bravest men ever, thought he should also be put forward for at least a George Cross. He just told us to forget it, he wasn't interested. It was all over and done with as far as he was concerned. Caroline, you have a father of whom you can be justly proud, a very brave, clever man, who could have gone places, but because of the terrible things he saw, and experienced, during the war decided he just wanted to spend the rest of his life as a quiet family man.'

Caroline felt close to tears, as a wave of emotion swept through her, at the thought of how her dear father had been so courageous, and never even mentioned it.

'That sounds very impressive, I must meet him, Caroline,' Billy said, looking all keen and interested.

Caroline looked at him and thought how typical of this man, not at all interested in her dad when he was just a good father, and schoolteacher, but now that he'd turned into a war hero, Billy had just got to meet him.

The talk went back to general topics including a discussion of what Caroline and Billy should do the next day. It was decided that, if it was another nice hot day, they should spend it in the family boat on Loch Ness.

As the men were having a last nightcap, Elizabeth and Caroline went upstairs together. Stopping outside Caroline's room, Elizabeth said, 'Alexander and I are very pleased Billy brought you up here for the weekend. It's so nice to see him with someone like you instead of his usual flighty popsies. I realise you haven't known him for long, and I can see he irritates you at times, but do try and persevere with him. He's really an awfully nice man.' Elizabeth kissed her on the cheek, said goodnight and went off to her own room.

Caroline wasted no time getting into bed. She lay in the darkened room with her mind in a turmoil. What a day! And now this, Lord and Lady Grant liked, and approved of her, and she'd imagined that they must have marked her down as most unsuitable for Billy. Well, anyway, in her own estimation, he was unsuitable for her, but it was really nice to have Alexander and Elizabeth Grant as friends, they were both so genuine and nice.

Was it? Yes, it was. Her bedroom door was being opened! She lay in the dark and started to breathe heavily and evenly. Someone came into the room, and a voice, Billy's of course, whispered, 'Caroline, are you awake?' She continued her breathing, and then heard him close the door as he crept out. She stuffed her head in the pillow and laughed as silently as she could. 'Oh, Billy, Billy,' she giggled. He really was rather sweet, in a funny sort of way.

Caroline was woken at seven in the morning by a sound that at first she couldn't place, then she realised what it was—bagpipes. She jumped out of bed and, looking out of the window, she could see MacDonald marching back and forth in front of the castle. It was pure magic to her. It was another gorgeous morning, and the sights and sounds made her want to pinch herself. She felt like a small child again, bursting with excitement. *Heavens,* she thought, *Scotland must be doing me good. I've not felt like this for years and years.*

Caroline and Billy had a quick breakfast and left for Loch Ness and the boat. The Range Rover seemed to be full of picnic baskets, bottles of wine etc., and Caroline had all sorts of kit, as Elizabeth had insisted on lending her sweaters, and raincoats, "just in case the weather changes". She felt equipped for any emergency.

Billy was in very good form and, after saying how much he'd enjoyed the previous day, kept her amused with stories of escapades he and his friends had got up to during their school holidays at the castle. When she asked about the bagpipes being played in the morning, he explained that that only happened when his father was in residence. It all sounded to her a bit like *royalty*. He also explained that MacDonald had played longer than usual on her side of the castle obviously in her honour, which had amused the family.

'It's a long time since he's taken to anyone the way he has to you. It's a big compliment; he's very suspicious and choosey.'

Not nearly as suspicious or choosey as you, thought Caroline.

Billy pulled the car off the road and drove down a short track to the Loch edge where there was a boathouse and landing stage.

'There she is, *Lake Windrush*'s her name,' he said as they stopped beside quite a large boat. 'It's a Broom 37, built in the early sixties, mahogany on oak. We bought her when I was waiting to go to Sandhurst and completely restored her. Wait till you get aboard, she beautifully fitted out. I've spent many a long day working on her and then sailing around in her. MacDonald was my main helpmate. He's a great jack-of-all-trades. Plenty of deck space if you want to sit in the sun.'

He showed her round, pointing out the work they'd done, and she had to agree it was a beautiful boat, with all its rich mahogany and fittings. When he'd got their belongings stowed away, he called out boyishly, 'All ashore that's going ashore. Stand by to cast off.' Then they were away with a purposeful burbling noise from the engines.

Caroline was dispatched to the galley to make coffee, and soon they were sipping it in the wheelhouse as they talked and laughed together. She thought how nice he seemed this morning, much more, what was it, relaxed perhaps?

'There's a small promontory of land with an old ruin on it, that's where I'm making for. We should get there just at the right time for lunch, and it won't be too far to get back afterwards. If we can be home by about five, we can have a cup of tea and still have plenty of time to relax and change before dinner.'

'That's sounds lovely, Billy. You're spoiling me and

giving me such a nice time. I do appreciate it.'

'What's a beautiful young woman for, if not to spoil? Anyway, it's fun having you up here, and it's good to bring someone that, for once, Father and Elizabeth don't look down their noses at. I'm glad you're enjoying yourself, and what do you think of Scotland, what little you've seen of it?'

'Oh, I think it's beautiful and your castle is unbelievable.'

'Yes, I think so too, but maybe you'd not like it quite so much in the dead of winter. It can be fairly cold and bleak then.' He took out some cushions so that Caroline could sit on the deck in the sun.

They passed the odd boat but there were not many about as the season was almost finished. Now and then, Billy would shout out about something they were passing that he thought might be of interest, otherwise the only sounds were the chugging of the engine, and the gurgling of water. Caroline's spirits were high, she was warm from the sun and full of good fresh air. She was also full of anticipation. What was the dinner party going to be like tonight, what would happen during the rest of the weekend, and most importantly, how was her relationship with Billy going to progress?

'That's were we're going to tie up for lunch. Can you see the old ruin?'

Billy manoeuvred the boat alongside a small jetty in a cove beneath the grassy hill, upon which stood the ruin, lit up in the sunshine.

'What a fantastic spot.'

'Yes, it used to be my favourite one for picnics when I was a boy. Lunch on the boat or on land?'

'Oh! Let's set it on the grass. It will most probably be the last chance for an outside picnic this year. Let's take advantage of it.'

The picnic basket turned out to contain wonderful cold salmon, salads, French bread, and things like homemade cold apple tart and fresh fruit. There was champagne, that had been well cooled in the boat's fridge, and at the end of the meal Billy went on board and made fresh coffee.

When they'd finished, Caroline felt content, and quite sleepy with food and fresh air—not to mention the champagne!

She lay back on the grass and closed her eyes. In an instant she felt Billy's lips on hers, they felt warm and sensuous. She responded to his kisses, and letting her lips part, allowed their tongues to meet. It was delicious, and she didn't attempt to stop him when his hand moved to her breast and stroked it through her silk shirt. She sighed and thought it was lucky she hadn't worn a bra. Then his hand was inside her shirt and his fingers were caressing and squeezing her rock-hard nipples. She felt hot waves of passion surging through her as his hard body pressed against hers. She just didn't care now what her resolve had been, she wanted him to make hard, passionate love to her, right there and then.

'Hello there, *Lake Windrush* ... Hello there, *Lake Windrush*!'

Her mind was too confused at first to even think what was happening, all she wanted was to be made love to. Then Billy moved away from her and stood up and she realised that someone was shouting to them. She did up her blouse, straightened her skirt and stood up. Her mind was still spinning with desire, but she could make out someone coming towards them in a small rowboat.

When the boat was alongside, the young man in it said, 'I'm terribly sorry to disturb you, but the engine on our boat has broken down, and we're stranded about a mile or so out on the Loch. I wondered if you could do something to help us?'

'Yes, of course,' said Billy. 'Tie your dingy onto the

back of my boat while I clear our stuff away and then we'll go out and collect your boat.'

'I say, thanks very much, very decent of you.'

Phew! Very decent of you too, thought Caroline as her racing heart began to slow down. *A few more minutes, and I'd have been another scalp on Billy's belt.* What did annoy her, though, was that Billy, instead of appearing crestfallen at having been interrupted at the crucial moment, seemed to be enjoying the prospect of *rescuing* a ship in distress.

When they found the boat, and had a tow rope on it, it was decided to tow it back to Billy's mooring as the easiest way of handling the situation. From there, someone could be contacted to see to the engine repairs, and the young family could stay aboard until they were mobile again.

When Caroline and Billy were in the Range Rover on their way back to the castle, the only comment Billy made about their passionate interlude was something like, 'a pity we'd been interrupted just as we were about to have some fun'. Caroline was not very impressed by this comment, and it made her, in retrospect, even more pleased that the man in the boat had arrived when he did.

With all this rescuing of boats, by the time they got back to the castle it was already twenty past six, and everyone was beginning to get worried that they had had a mishap.

There was an urgent message for Billy to ring his office, and although tea was long finished, another pot was sent for so that Caroline could have a cup before going up to change. While she was sipping her tea, she told Elizabeth what a super day she'd had, and about the rescue.

Elizabeth laughed. 'That's Billy, things always happen wherever he is. He just seems to be a magnet for excitement and trouble, admittedly part of it is because of his job, but the rest just happens for no apparent reason.'

Billy came in looking annoyed, and more like his London self. 'I'm sorry, Caroline, we've got to go back tomorrow instead of Monday.'

'Oh, Billy, that's a pity, I thought Caroline would be able to share one of our nice lazy Sundays.'

'We won't have to leave until mid-afternoon, but I must be in London very early Monday morning. I'm sorry, it just can't be helped.'

Caroline was surprised how sorry she felt as she was really enjoying being with the Grants and already though of Elizabeth as a good friend. She would have been happy to stay with them much longer than this, even without Billy.

When she was in her room, she saw that she'd got just about an hour before they all met up for drinks at eight. With the rush, she hadn't found out much about the dinner party—Who was coming? How many people etc?—but she was looking forward to it, and was certain it was going to be fun.

After a quick bath—she would have liked to lie and soak, and to think about her day with Billy—she massaged her body with L'Air du Temps. She spent some time on her hair, which she decided didn't look too bad, considering she'd spent the day on a boat, and rolling about in the grass with Billy!

This evening she was going to try, for the first time, some Divinaura by Guerlain, which was meant "to create a complexion glowing with light and health". With her eyes and lips also made-up, and wearing only her wispy silk Charnos briefs, she stood back and surveyed herself in the mirror. *Not bad, not bad at all,* she decided. She giggled away as she wondered what Billy would say, or do, if he could see her like this. *There'd be no holding him in then,* she thought, *unless perhaps somebody suddenly need rescuing or something!*

With sheer tights and high-heeled, black, satin slingbacks on she was ready for the new Ralph Lauren velvet shift dress. When it was on, she looked at herself again. The girls in the shop were right, it had a very subtle, sexy look. Was it a bit too revealing? No ... no ... no. She loved it; it was terrific. All she needed now was a little more of the perfume she always wore, Chanel's "Coco", and she was ready for anything. She found she was laughing again. What was the matter with her? She was meant to be a serious-minded, virtually on-the-shelf widow, struggling to earn her living in the hard journalistic world, and now all she seemed to do was cavort round castles, and roll about in the grass with handsome, rich young men.

She was still laughing as she started to descend the main staircase when she suddenly realised that the hall was full of people, and that they were all looking up at her. She tried to compose her face and to look serious. As she reached the bottom stair, a young man stepped forward and took her hand as though to assist her down the last step. 'You're a vision out of the sky. I can't believe you are real. Who are you? Where do you come from and why, oh why, haven't I met you before?'

'Because you're an old Highland clodhopper, and don't deserve to meet charming, beautiful, desirable young ladies like Caroline. Caroline, this is Andrew Campbell who people, when we were young, used to mistakenly call my best friend. My advice is to keep well away from him as he is highly dangerous. Andrew, this is Caroline Dalglish, a friend from the south who is very, very intelligent and renowned for being able to spot an unprincipled rake a mile off.'

'Thank you for those few kind words, Billy, but I'm sure that Caroline will appreciate that they're all false and only an attempt to hold a good man at bay.'

Andrew was a very attractive man, even taller than Billy, with black curly hair and green eyes. He and Billy carried on pulling each other's leg in an amusing way for a few minutes until Billy said he must take Caroline round to meet the others.

There seemed to be about twenty or thirty people, the men were all wearing dinner jackets, except one or two who were in dress kilts, and the women were very smartly dressed. The numbers were fairly evenly divided between the various age groups. They all seemed charming to Caroline, and she thought how lucky the Grants were to have so many nice friends living in the vicinity. Lord Grant made a big fuss of her, and told everyone how clever she was, and what she did. Quite a few of them knew her name and had even read some of her work.

Caroline was just having a few words with Elizabeth

when in through the door came a late arrival. Caroline looked and then looked again. It was a stunning girl. She was about five feet five or six with black, shortish hair parted on the left and then swept across her head where it kinked coquettishly. Caroline couldn't see the colour of her eyes, but they were large, and sparkling, and she had a "Bridget Bardot" mouth. She was dressed in what Caroline could only describe as a fantastic outfit. It had a multi-coloured silk damask jacket, with a gold collar, and a miniskirt in matching gold. Her high-heeled black courts showed off her long legs to perfection. Everybody was calling out hello to her, and it was obvious that she was extremely popular. She made straight for Billy, and they hugged and kissed, a bit more than necessary, Caroline thought.

'That's Fiona, Andrew's sister, and the third member of, "the three musketeers", as they were known when they were kids. I think you'll like her,' Elizabeth said, looking straight at Caroline.

I'm not too sure I will, thought Caroline, as she looked across the room at this devastating girl, still hanging onto Billy.

At that moment, Emanuel, the Grants' Spanish butler, came in to announce dinner. Billy seemed too busy with

Fiona to come and take Caroline through to the Great Hall, but Andrew was there in a flash, offering her his arm.

The Great Hall looked magnificent with the long central table set with silver and crystal glass, and as the evenings were now getting a bit cooler, there was a log fire burning in the fireplace at each end of the hall. 'I hope we're sitting next to each other, Caroline, but if old Billy's had anything to do with it, I'll bet we're not. Not that I can blame him if he has, I'd have done the same to him, given half a chance.'

They found Caroline's place, which to her surprise was on Lord Grant's right. Andrew's guess had been correct, he was seated miles away. 'Oh damn!' he said. 'Never mind, we can get together after dinner. How long are you up here for, a week or so?'

'No, going back tomorrow after lunch.'

'I say, that's a bit off, isn't it? I'll have to follow you to London then.'

'I don't live in London, in Oxford,' replied Caroline, laughing.

'That's even better. I can come down and visit my old college.'

'Come on, Andrew, do you mind going to your seat

and not holding everyone up?' interrupted Billy as he came striding up.

'I don't know how you put up with him, Caroline. He seems to get ruder and more unpleasant as he gets older,' said Andrew as he moved off, grinning.

What a dinner. They started with smoked salmon, and then had some wonderful dish prepared for grouse, shot on their own grouse moors of course, herbs and wine and things. Caroline thought it delicious. This was followed by a choice of fresh fruit salad or lemon meringue, and then great boards containing mountains of different kinds of cheese were put on the table.

All through the meal, wine and conversation flowed unchecked. Billy was sitting on Caroline's right, and Andrew's mother was opposite her. Caroline could see where Fiona got her dark liquid beauty.

During dinner, Lord Grant talked quite a bit with Caroline, asking her more questions about her life, and her parents. He was really pleased to hear that her father and mother were now happily installed in a Cornish cottage. He told her that he would very much like to see her father again and suggested that if ever her parents were visiting Scotland, then they should come and spend a few days at the castle. He carried on by saying, 'It's funny that Billy mentioned recently that his company does some work for a man that both your father and I knew during the war. When you give your father my message you must mention to him, as I'm sure it will amuse him, that Billy does work for that old rogue Alastair Brown, who is still playing funny games, although he must by now be quite an age.'

Caroline didn't know what to say, should she tell Lord Grant her connection with Alastair or shouldn't she?

Billy had obviously overhead what his father had said, and realising her predicament, interrupted, 'Excuse me butting in, but while I remember, Father, are you and Elizabeth still planning on coming to London during October?'

When they were leaving the table after dinner, Lord Grant took Caroline's hand and kissed it. 'It gave me great pleasure having you sit next to me at dinner. You are so beautiful and look so like Elizabeth did at your age. I think you also have something else in common, you're both extremely intelligent and know what is the right thing.'

'Thank you,' murmured Caroline, thinking, *And what did he mean by that?* Did he know about her job for Alastair Brown and was saying she should know better? Or was he indicating that she would be silly to get any serious ideas about Billy? Or was he just being nice? If it was the Alastair affair, then she knew he was right, but she was still going to do it. If it were Billy he was referring to—no problem. The last thing she intended was to get any serious thoughts about the Honourable Mr William Grant.

Billy grabbed her hand. 'Come on, we're going to dance in the hall. I want to see if everything is ready.'

While they were having dinner, a four-piece band had set up in the main hall, and it started to play as they came through. The chandelier had been turned off, and with just the bracket lights, there was a pleasant, diffused light. It really had the atmosphere of a small intimate club.

'What do you think?'

'It's terrific, Billy. It's got real atmosphere.'

'Good. What about some coffee before we start to dance?'

'Fine.'

Coffee was being served in the sitting room, and there was a bar in what Caroline now called *the small dining room.*

As they sat having coffee, they were joined by Andrew and Fiona Campbell. Close up, Caroline realised that Fiona was even more beautiful than she had appeared at first sight. 'I don't think you two have been introduced yet, Fiona arriving last, and late, as usual.'

From the way Billy said this, and from the way Fiona answered, it was obvious to Caroline that these two knew each other extremely well. Was it just because of their childhood together, or was it more?

As they were introduced, Caroline felt herself under close scrutiny, and got the impression that Fiona was not overly pleased to find her here.

'I've never heard Billy mention you before. Have you known each other long?'

'No, but then I've never heard him mention you, and I believe you must have known him for years.' *I shouldn't have said that,* thought Caroline.

'Yes, we've been the closest of friends for a very long time. Billy, stop talking to Andrew and dance with me.'

'I was just going to dance with Caroline.'

'No, go on, you dance with her. I want to dance with Caroline,' said Andrew, taking her hand and leading her towards the Great Hall. Caroline and Billy's eyes met, and she could see he was slightly annoyed at not being able to dance with her. Andrew was a good dancer and clearly enjoyed it. 'Have you known Billy long?'

'No, barely a week.'

'Good Lord! He's a jolly fast worker, got you up here

for the weekend already. I wish I knew how he does it. I never know what to say to girls.'

Caroline laughed. 'Oh, yes, Andrew, quite, that's obvious. Do you live up here all the time?'

'No, I'm in the army. Billy and I went in together. Then the silly old sod has a row and leaves, and I'm stuck. My father would kill me if I resigned my commission and went to join Billy in his security company. I'd like to do it, but I just can't at the moment.'

They danced on for a while and Caroline thought what a very nice, and amusing man he was. She could see Billy and Fiona dancing, though they seemed more engrossed in whatever they were saying to each other.

Looking up at Andrew, she said, 'I believe you three have been very good friends since you were kids.'

'We certainly have, and still are, although things have changed a bit now.'

'What, because of you and Billy not being in the army together anymore?'

'Good Lord no. Billy and I are just as close as ever, even if we don't see each other as much as we used to.'

'Oh!' said Caroline and left it at that.

After dancing for a while, they went and got a drink and took it into the drawing room where they sat in comfort, and comparative quiet. Andrew was just telling her a story about a party he and Billy had recently been to when Billy came in looking for her.

'Come on, Caroline, what about that dance?'

'Let me just finish my drink and rest for a minute, then I'm yours to command.'

'That sounds all right, Billy, lucky chap. Think I'll leave you to it and see if I can find myself a willing maiden to dance the night away with. See you later.'

When Andrew had gone, Caroline asked, 'What happened to Fiona, is she dancing with someone else?'

'No, she's gone home in a huff.'

'Oh dear! I'm sorry.'

'Don't be, she's like that. There's nothing really between us, but whenever we meet, she always seems to expect that she is the most important person in my life. We're very good, long-standing friends, but as far as I'm concerned, that's all there is to it. Her parents are also very keen that we should get together in a permanent way, so it can be a bit difficult at times.'

'She's certainly a very attractive girl, one of the most beautiful I've ever met.'

'Yes, apart from you, I can't think of one more beautiful.'

'Billy, you're too kind. I don't think I can compete with her.'

'Oh yes you can, quite different, of course, one very dark and one very blonde. I've always been a sucker for blondes myself. Incidentally, my old dad is very taken with you. Apart from Elizabeth, he tells me you're the most attractive woman he's seen for years. What with that, and our old misogynist MacDonald falling under your spell, not to mention Andrew, you've done rather well in your two days north of the border.'

'You're an awful leg-puller. I must say, though, I do like your father, he's a really nice man and very attractive.'

'Not bad, particularly when you remember he's in his late sixties. I can hear the band is playing some smoochy music. Let's go and dance. I want to hold you in my arms.'

'An offer I can't refuse.'

They went into the hall where more lights had been turned off until it was extremely dim, and Billy took her in his arms. Caroline felt great. She was on an all-time high. This was going to be a few days she would never forget. She had to swallow hard as she suddenly felt her emotions welling up inside her. Here she was in the arms of one of the handsomest men she'd ever met; dancing to soft romantic music in a castle that was absolute magic.

A slight cold chill ran through her, for a split second, as she wondered if she was suddenly going to wake up and find that it was all just a dream. Those arms encircling her were real enough, as was the hard body pressed against her. She looked up to say how wonderful it all was, but before she could utter a word, Billy's lips had found hers in another of those divine kisses of his. They stayed on the floor just rocking gently to the music with their bodies close.

Caroline lost track of time. She was warm and moist with desire. Billy stopped rocking to the music and kissed her once again then he whispered, 'Darling, we're the only ones still dancing. I think we'll have to finish and let the band go.'

With regret she moved out of his arms, and for a moment, felt quite weak with emotion and desire. They held hands walking over to thank, and say goodnight to, the band.

Although they hadn't noticed it, most people had already gone, but the Grants, and the Campbells were still in the drawing room. When Billy and Caroline walked in, hand-in-hand, Alexander Grant called out, 'Come on you two, you're just in time for a glass of champagne to finish the evening.'

Getting to his feet, General Sir Ian Campbell said to his wife, 'Come along, my dear, we must go. Ready, Andrew?' They said their farewells and thanks, but, with the exception of Andrew, not very enthusiastically to Caroline.

When the Campbells had gone, the family had a good old laugh about what people had said and done during the evening. Caroline was amused. They might be aristocracy, living in a castle, but they were just as gossipy as anyone else.

'I though old Campbell seemed a bit grumpy at the end of the evening,' Lord Grant said, sipping his champagne.

'I think he was annoyed about Fiona,' replied Elizabeth.

'What, because she went so early?'

'No, silly, because Billy was making more of a fuss of Caroline than he was of her.'

'I don't know, it's all too complicated for me. After all, Caroline's Billy's weekend guest, and Fiona is just the girl next door. So, who should he have been looking after?'

Elizabeth and Billy thought that very funny, but Caroline felt a bit embarrassed if she'd caused any trouble between two such old friends.

They continued to talk for a while as they finished their champagne, then Elizabeth said, 'I'm for bed.'

They all went upstairs together, and Billy had to say his goodnights at the top of the stairs as his room was in another part of the castle, but the other three were down the same corridor. He kissed Elizabeth on the cheek, and then turned to Caroline and kissed her on the lips. She wished they'd been alone as she would have liked more than that.

When they reached Caroline's door, Elizabeth gave her a hug and kiss on the cheek, and Lord Grant did the same.

With goodnights ringing in Caroline's ears, she went into her room and shut her door. One bedside light was on, and her bed was turned back with her nightdress—she'd thought she'd better bring one—laid across it. *God!* she thought, *It's going to take me some time to get back to normal living after all this.* Worst of all, she was going to miss Billy being around all the time. She'd been wrong. He wasn't the hard, egotistical man she'd thought him. Seeing him in this new light, she could even fall in love with him.

She kicked off her shoes, pulled off her tights and briefs, and carefully lifted her dress over her head. As she was doing so, she heard the door open and shut. Turning, she found Billy standing grinning at her. Holding her dress in front of her naked body, questions flashed through her mind. Would she be stupid to give up her resolve not to let him make love to her? Did she really want him, or was it just that she was starved of physical love? Was there any reason why they should not enjoy each other after such a romantic day together? She made her decision—yes, she would—but she would make him woo her a bit more first.

'What on earth are you doing in my room, Billy?'

'I came because I knew you wanted me to.'

He stepped forward and his arms were round her. His warm hands travelled down her bare back and ended caressing her bottom. Through her mind flashed the memory of him feeling her bottom that day at the embassy, she tried to step back and her dress that had been between them slipped to the floor. He let go and, standing back, let his eyes move slowly over her body. 'You're absolutely divine. I want you, every little bit of you.'

She wanted him too, now almost desperately, but she thought she'd just make him try that little bit harder. 'No, Billy, I don't think I can, please go.'

Then he made a terrible mistake. Stepping forward, he took hold of her shoulders and, looking into her eyes, said, 'Come on, darling, let's get to bed and stop all this chatter. After all, you're not some little virgin, but a mature, experienced woman. You know you want it as much as I do, and anyway, I'll bet you only came up here to get laid.'

Caroline gasped. She couldn't believe it. He was what she'd thought he was when they first met. She struggled away from him, managed to pick up her dress and hold it in front of herself. Then in a choked voice, she gasped, 'Get out of my room. GET OUT!'

He stood looking at her with a surprised expression on his face and didn't move.

Caroline walked past him and holding open the door said, in a calmer voice, 'Please get out right now, and stay out.'

'But I only ...'

'GET OUT!'

He went and she shut the door as tears started to run down her cheeks.

CHAPTER SIX

Caroline had a bad night. When she first got into bed, she lay in the dark and felt tears run down her cheeks. Her mind was full of a mixture of anger and disappointment. She'd wondered why Billy had invited her to Scotland, and now she knew why. It was purely because he fancied her sexually. He had no respect for her. She was now certain he had no intention of a lasting friendship of any kind. All he wanted was a few days' fun rolling about in her bed.

She had to admit that she'd wanted him to make love to her, wanted it desperately, but to be just purely physical was not enough for her. When he said what he said, it had the same effect as if a bucket of icy water had been thrown over her. To crown it all, when he left her room, he just walked out with his normal, nonchalant, arrogant manner.

Everything had happened so quickly. She couldn't believe that they'd known each other only five days—*five days*—that was ridiculous; during that time her emotions had ranged between hate and something almost akin to love.

How was it, she wondered, *that someone with such great parents could be so ill-mannered and chauvinistic? But then, of course, Elizabeth was only his stepmother—it must all come from his own mother.*

As she lay there turning thoughts over and over in her mind she began to wonder if perhaps she was being stupid about the whole thing. Was it just that she didn't understand Billy's type or his way life. It couldn't be more different to what she'd been used to with John. Good, kind, considerate John who would never have forced her to do anything she didn't want to, but then she had to remember that he hadn't satisfied her because he was too much the other way. Perhaps, after all, it was all her. Was there something basically wrong with her? Was there just no satisfying her? Perhaps she would never be happy with anyone. As the night wore on, her thoughts got blacker and blacker. By dawn she was picturing herself, in years to come, a little old grey lady living on her own, with no friends, and coming to the end of a completely unfulfilled life. Then she fell into a troubled sleep.

Caroline was woken by the skirl of the pipes at eight the next morning. She lay there for a while trying to work out where she was, then she remembered, and what had happened the night before. She was feeling more philosophical than she had during the night and was even able to smile about her "old age" syndrome. After all, what was Billy to her? If she didn't like him, so what, there were plenty of other men around if that's what she wanted. One thing, however, she was quite clear on, was that she did not want to go to San Francisco with him. San Francisco—she'd almost forgotten all about that, with all the other drama that was going on.

When she got out of bed, she drew the curtains and looked out. It was another lovely morning, but with a hazy sun, and a slight mist. It was autumn, and no longer summer. She had a cold shower to refresh her, and to wash away the night's blues, and then put on her new Episode trouser suit with a silk and mohair turtleneck sweater. As it was now nearly nine, she left her room and went downstairs wondering how to treat Billy.

When she went into the breakfast room, Elizabeth was sitting on her own, reading the Sunday papers. Getting up, she embraced Caroline, kissed her on her cheek, and looking hard at her, asked, 'Did you sleep well?'

'Yes, fine thanks,' Caroline replied as she helped herself to cornflakes and coffee.

'Alexander has taken Billy off to show him a new plantation that is being started this autumn. He wanted to take you as well, but I thought you'd rather have a quiet morning, as you have to fly back today.'

'Yes, it'll be lovely to spend the morning here.'

'Caroline, I hope you won't think me interfering, but is everything all right? I was coming back to your room, last night, to tell you breakfast was not until nine on Sundays, and I couldn't help overhearing your row with Billy. You don't have to talk about it if you don't want to, but I'm very angry with him if he caused you any distress, particularly as it was here in our home. If you want to talk, please do, otherwise just tell me to mind my own business.'

'Please don't be angry with him. I'm sure it was

my fault that a misunderstanding occurred. You see, Elizabeth, although I'm very much out in the world with my job, and have to be able to look after myself, I'm not very experienced as far as men are concerned. I started to work for John as soon as I got my degree, and eighteen months later I married him. Then he was killed in that terrible accident just over two years ago, and I've only just started to get over it during the last few months. So, apart from the odd flirtation with other students when I was at college, I've only ever had one man in my life. John was quite different from anyone like Billy, and although he wasn't much older than him, he seemed so. He was actually ten years older that me, but because he was such a brilliant academic nearly all his friends, and therefore mine, were much, much older. John was also a very sincere man, and never tried to lead you on or tell you anything except the absolute truth. So, I'm still taken unawares when someone, in my personal life, does. There is also another reason that perhaps makes it difficult for Billy and me to understand one another, and that's his background. I was brought up in a small town, in a small house, in a family that, although not impoverished, had to be careful what they spent. To sum up, I've spent a very dull, middle-class life, whereas Billy is an aristocrat who has had, and is still having, a very exciting life. In all ways we're poles apart, it was stupid of me to come here, anything that happened is my own fault.'

'Oh, Caroline, don't feel like that, in a lot of ways you're quite wrong. If there's any trouble between you, I'm sure it's nothing to do with your background. The main problem is with Billy, and what happened when he was just a small boy. He has never forgotten it or got over it. You may already know that his mother ran away with another man when Billy was about six. It was terrible, both Alexander and Billy adored her, and she went without even saying goodbye. She just left a note, not saying who she'd gone with, or where she'd gone to. It was six months or so before Alexander found out all the details, by which time he'd got over it a little, but not enough to stop him wanting revenge. You see, these Grants are descended from old Highland warrior stock, and their motto, roughly translated, means "no man touches me or mine with impunity". It's like something out of a book what happened next. Evidently, Alexander was about to follow the couple to Argentina, to deal with them in his own way, when MacDonald, with the help of some of his lads, grabbed him, and locked him down in one of the old dungeons. They wouldn't let him out until he'd calmed down and promised to leave well alone. All this time poor little Billy was grief-stricken and asking for his Mummy. At last Alexander had to tell him that she'd gone and would never be coming back. From that moment on, Billy has never been able to trust a woman or consider her as anything than a passing amusement. Even with me, it was years after I'd married Alexander before Billy trusted me. That's why we were surprised, and pleased, when he arrived with you. We thought that perhaps he'd changed at last, as normally he only brings up girls who are fairly empty-headed and are just out for a bit of fun.'

'Thank you for telling me. It's so kind of you to take such an interest. I feel, however, that there's no possible future for me with Billy, even if he did care for me as a person, and not just as someone to have fun in bed with.'

'I think you're being a bit hard on yourself, and on Billy. Why don't you think there can be anything more lasting between the two of you? Is it that you've come to the conclusion that you don't really like him that much?'

'No, I didn't mean it like that. I just meant that obviously I don't have the background to be considered, by any of you, as the right permanent partner for him.'

'I wouldn't be too sure about that. Admittedly, Alexander's first wife was an Earl's daughter, but when I first met him, I was an ex-fashion model struggling to become a dress-designer. My father, who is not much older than my husband, was retired from the Indian Army, where he was a colonel, at the time of independence. He and my mother live in a Shropshire cottage on a small pension, and a few investments. Not a dissimilar background to your own, is it?'

Caroline sat for a minute looking at Elizabeth. She was amazed. Elizabeth was so much to "the manner born" it didn't seem possible that she'd not been brought up as a member of some grand family. 'I must admit I'm surprised, even though you're always so kind, and charming, you've that sort of inborn grand manner.'

Elizabeth laughed. 'There you are then, that's what happens when you live for a long time with someone as wonderful as Alexander.'

'Yes, I see what you mean. I suppose my trouble is that I'm just completely mixed up. One minute I almost hate Billy and the next I almost love him. All this when I haven't known him for a whole week yet. Incidentally, did you ever hear how we first met a couple of months ago? No ... well, let me tell you.'

When Caroline had finished describing the *fateful day* at the embassy, Elizabeth laughed out loud. 'I'm sorry,' she choked, 'but I can just picture it all, and knowing the people concerned, I can see the funny side.'

Caroline, for a second or two, was quite upset at Elizabeth's reaction, and then she caught the infectious laugh, and started herself. It was the first time she'd seen anything even remotely funny about what happened, but now she wondered why she hadn't found it laughable from the beginning.

'I'm so sorry, Caroline, but the thought of poor little you being *frisked* by Billy while big Fred, and what must have been enormous Stan, held you spread-eagled was just too much. Mind you, if it'd happened to me, I'd have been just as shocked, and enraged as you were. I'd be prepared to bet, however, that Billy didn't really notice anything about your body. When he frisked you he would have been, as he said, just looking for weapons or explosives. Poor you, what an awful thing to happen. To add injury to insult, you didn't even get your interview.'

'No, but the Arabs did give me compensation to make up for all the hassle, which was nice and, between you and me, allowed me to help my parents buy a conservatory they wanted.'

'It all came out rather well then, except for your having been outraged by Billy's behaviour. I don't know how to advise you, even if you want my advice, but if I was in your shoes, I think I'd just play it a bit cool.'

'Yes, I think you're right, but I don't know if I can forgive him for last night. It's not his coming into my room or anything, but because of his attitude, and because he'd obviously just marked me down as another of his "play girls" who would be quite happy to jump into bed with him whenever he wanted. I do find him very attractive, and I'll admit, Elizabeth, I'd have slept with him last night if he'd approached me with love and respect. I'm not a person interested in sex for sex's sake, and I'm hurt that he should think so.'

'Yes, I know exactly what you're saying. If only Billy could get over this distrust of women, then I'm sure everything would be fine. At the moment, I'm not sure that he ever will. What it really needs is a situation where a woman proves that the female sex can be trusted beyond question, and I can't really see how that can come about. Perhaps, Caroline, in the circumstances, the best advice is for you to forget Billy if you don't just want a physical relationship and to find someone who can also give you emotionally what you need and require.'

Caroline was shocked by this. It was basically what she had been saying to herself, but now it was out in the open, it was difficult to appreciate that perhaps she should give up and forget all about Billy. Her mind was in turmoil. She just couldn't seem to think straight. Billy had upset her equilibrium and she'd not been the same rational, hard-working person she'd been before he'd arrived on the scene. He'd broken her out of her dull-thinking rut, but had he given her anything in its place? No, with regret, she didn't think he had. What was she going to do? Was she going to go back home and revert to what she'd been before his arrival? She remembered her dream of the night before. No, this mustn't happen. She must make her life fuller than it had been. She desperately needed a man again, both emotionally and sexually, but could this possibly be Billy? Had Elizabeth said something?

'I'm sorry, my mind was wandering,' she said.

'I only suggested we go out into the garden. It's nice and sunny, and fairly warm again, and they'll want to clear breakfast and lay lunch. You'll probably wish to pack before lunch as I imagine Billy will want to take off around three.'

The two women walked in the garden for a while, and Caroline realised how much she liked and admired Elizabeth. She was just how she'd like to be herself when she was in her mid-forties.

When she went up to pack, Caroline decided to stay in her Episode suit for the journey home as it was the only time she'd worn it this weekend. She hadn't even worn her fabulous new Louis Feraud suit at all. *Typical,* she thought. All that rushing into London to buy clothes, and she could quite well have got away with what she already had.

When she came downstairs just before one and went into the sitting room, Alexander and Billy were there having just arrived back from their morning trip. They both stood up and said, 'Hello.' Then Billy went off to, as he said, "freshen up".

Lord Grant offered Caroline a drink, and when he brought her a gin and tonic, said, 'Sorry you weren't with us this morning, but Elizabeth thought you'd rather spend it quietly here.'

'Yes, it was nice to have a chance to chatter, and to look round the garden. I'm only sorry I won't have time to see everything else.'

'Well, next time, my dear, as I shall insist on your coming up here to stay with us again. If Billy doesn't ask you again fairly soon, you chase him up about it, as both Elizabeth and I want to see you again.'

'That's awfully kind of you. I shall look forward to it very much. It's been a fantastic weekend for me, so nice to meet you both, and to be made to feel so welcome.'

'I do hope you and Billy become really good friends as, between you and me, I'm pretty appalled by the young women he usually brings up here. It would be nice if he'd concentrate a bit more on a respectable, intelligent girl like you. After all, he is in his thirties, and it's time he became a bit more respectable.'

Caroline didn't know what to say, she was very surprised and flattered that he should have made her his confidante. She was saved from answering as Elizabeth came in at that moment to be offered, and to accept, a pre-luncheon drink. She was closely followed by Billy.

Looking at him, Caroline wondered how on earth she was going to be able to stop seeing him. As he came in smiling, she decided he was definitely the handsomest, and most attractive man she'd ever met. Just looking at him gave her an ache in the pit of her stomach, and sent a wave of almost nausea through her.

In other words, he made her feel quite randy, and this was just not on, she must get better control of herself.

Smiling at her as though nothing had happened between them, Billy said, 'All packed and ready for a three o'clock take-off?'

'Yes, I'm ready whenever you are.'

During lunch Elizabeth mentioned to Billy that Andrew Campbell had phoned to talk to him. 'Does he want me to ring him before I go?' he asked.

'No, it's not necessary,' she said, smiling at Caroline. 'He only wanted Caroline's phone number, so I was able to give it to him.'

'What the devil did he want that for?' growled Billy.

'Well, I should imagine so that he can phone her.'

'I don't think that's a very good idea. He's a very wild chap, old Andrew.'

Elizabeth and Andrew exchanged a smile, and Caroline, smiling demurely, said, 'Oh, that'll be nice, I'll look forward to hearing from him, although, I don't expect he gets down south very often.'

'He is in fact stationed down there, isn't he, Billy?'

'Yes, he's still in Hereford.'

'He's quite close then. That's a very easy drive from Oxford.'

The three of them were rather enjoying baiting Billy who, unlike his usual quick-witted self, seemed to fall for it. *Why, in any case,* wondered Caroline, *was he worried or even interested in who called her, or for that matter, dated her?* It seemed as if, perhaps, he was as confused as she was.

After lunch it was time to gather their things together and say their goodbyes.

Lord Grant gave Caroline a warm hug and kissed her, saying, 'Don't forget to give my message to your father, nor that you're welcome here any time you can make it.'

Caroline thanked him warmly and then turned to Elizabeth. 'Thank you so much for having me, and for being so kind to me. I'll often think of you here in your lovely home.'

'It's been a real pleasure having you here, Caroline, and we mean what Alexander said, you'll always be welcome here, whether you come with Billy, or on your own.'

As they climbed into MacDonald's Range Rover, Caroline felt almost tearful. She couldn't think when she'd met people that she liked as much as the Grants. Without any great fuss or bother they'd made her feel completely at home, almost like one of the family. She wondered if she would ever come up to this lovely place again. Certainly, if she did, it wouldn't be with Billy.

Billy had obviously been to check the plane during the morning as when they reached the airship it was already out of the hanger. MacDonald helped with the cases, and everything was soon stowed in the plane. All that was left was to say goodbye to MacDonald, and they were ready for take-off.

Once airborne, Billy was jabbering away on the radio and was unable to speak to Caroline for a few minutes. 'Just had word that the weather is not so good around London, they've had a big thunderstorm, and a lot of rain. We wouldn't run into it until we're well down into the Midlands, but then it could become a bit bumpy. We've got tea in the thermoses so I suggest you dish it up in about an hour's time when things should still be calm.'

Elizabeth had given her the latest copy of *Vogue* to read on the journey, so Caroline buried herself in its pages. Then her eyes glazed, and her head nodded, and she had a little doze.

She was dreaming that she was swinging gently in a hammock, suspended between two apple trees, in a beautiful riverside garden when something seemed to shake her shoulder, and she could hear a distant voice calling her name. She opened her eyes—what was it—and where was she? It was Billy shaking her gently. 'Better get the tea now. We'll be running into the storm in ten minutes or so.'

Going back to the bar she found not only tea but also delicious-looking homemade cakes.

They only just had time to finish their tea before they ran into the storm.

Billy was looking quite serious as the plane bucked and rolled, forked lightning crackled around them, and sheets of rain cascaded onto the windscreen and side windows. To start with Caroline felt pretty nervous, but after a few minutes, much to her surprise, she began to feel, if anything, elated. Billy was wrestling with the controls, and almost constantly talking on the radio as they got deeper into the storm. Then he turned and shouted, 'Are you okay?'

She could see the look of surprise on his face as she smiled and shouted back, 'Yes, fine.'

It felt like being in a sailing dinghy running before the wind in a short, choppy sea. It got darker and darker and Caroline couldn't help but be impressed by the confident, efficient manner that the plane was being flown.

'Not long now and we'll be through the worst of it,' shouted Billy. But as he finished speaking, there was an awful bang. For a split second, the plane seemed to almost stop, and then there followed a loud clattering noise from the left-hand side of the aircraft, and it started to shudder in a big way. Caroline could see what looked like smoke coming from the engine on that side, but she wasn't too sure because of the heavy rain. Billy just seemed to be working like mad with the controls. He said nothing to her, nor did he have time to speak on the radio. At last, he turned his head, and looking directly at her with a very calm, reassuring half-smile, shouted above the increased din, 'Seem to have lost the port engine, must have been struck by lightning; nothing to worry about, this thing flies beautifully on one.'

'Good, I'm pleased about that,' she said, grinning at him. This time she could see the open astonishment on his face, and then he gave her a broad grin, and got back to his controls and radio.

The thing that surprised her the most was that she hadn't just made herself say that to reassure him, she meant it. She was, if anything, excited by the situation. She had complete faith in Billy's competence to get them out of this and down safely. Her main worry now was whether she would be able to remember all the details, without notes, as she was already planning a feature she was going to write concerning this experience. Her journalist instincts had got the better of any fear she might have felt. She watched Billy as he dealt with the controls, and she could tell that he was completely confident that he could handle the situation and, in fact, he was thoroughly enjoying the challenge of an emergency. She had to admire him, he was a real action man, which made it even worse that he was not for her. Even though she'd only known him for a few days, and then not intimately, she knew she was going to miss him a great deal.

He finished talking on the radio, and turning to her, shouted, 'They've cleared the runway for us at Birmingham. We'll be landing there in a couple of minutes. Can you move back into the main cabin and take up a crash position? ... Good—well done—I'll see you in a few minutes when we land. Be prepared to get out fast just in case of fire or anything.'

Caroline hung on to partitions and seats as she moved back into the main cabin. Sitting down she strapped herself in, and taking a cushion, she got into the emergency position, as taught on airliners.

It felt as if the plane was coming in sideways. It seemed to be travelling very fast. She wanted to look out one of the portholes, but she knew she must not. There was a big bump, and for a second it felt as though the plane was slewing round. Then it seemed to straighten, and to go along the runway, gradually slowing down.

As soon as they landed, Billy was beside her, releasing her safety belt, grabbing her arm and propelling her through the aircraft door. On the runway around them she could see fire engines, ambulances and lots of people, some of whom helped her from the plane, and into a waiting vehicle. It all seemed very exciting to be the centre of so much attention. As soon as Billy was seated beside her, they were driven off to the airport buildings, taken inside and given some coffee. Caroline, looking down at herself, found that her poor Episode suit, being worn for the first time, was soaking wet from the rain, and black from having brushed against the side of the plane as she got out.

Billy brought over a very nice, rugged-looking man that he'd been talking to, and who turned out to be the head of airport security, or something, and of course, an old friend of Billy's. Her bags had been put into a private office so that she could change out of her wet clothes before continuing her journey to Oxford. When she came out feeling dry and respectable again, Billy said, 'There's a chauffeur-driven car, waiting to take you to Oxford, as soon as you're ready.'

'That's quick, when did you arrange that?'

'On the radio, when we lost our port engine.'

Wow! thought Caroline. *There we were careening through an electric storm, with one engine gone, and this man calmly sits up there ordering chauffeur-driven cars.*

'I won't be travelling back with you, Caroline. I've got to stay here to organise the handling of the plane. I don't think it should be too long, and by then Fred, Stan or one of the other boys will be up here to collect me.'

'I suppose you arranged that on the plane's radio when you were ordering a car for me?'

'Yes, it seemed the most sensible thing to do. I didn't want you to have to hang about after what you'd gone through. I must congratulate you and say how impressed I was with the way you stood up to the ordeal. It was quite magnificent. I actually got the impression that you were, at one stage, almost enjoying it all.'

'Well, I wouldn't say that I'd want to do that sort of thing every day, but it wasn't too bad, and I had complete confidence in your being able to handle the situation.'

'That's very nice of you to say so. I appreciate it. Your case has been taken to the car. Are you all ready to go, or would you like some more coffee or something?'

'No, I'm fine.'

Caroline was becoming irritable at Billy's apparent lack of concern for her.

'I could be in Oxford by about ten-ish, shall I come and take you out to a late dinner?'

'No thank you, Billy. I shall want to have a bath, get unpacked and go to bed.'

'If you don't want dinner, I could still come and see you.'

'No thank you.'

'Okay, let's make it dinner tomorrow night?'

'No, I can't make it tomorrow.'

'So, shall we make it Tuesday?'

'No, Billy.'

'Are you trying to avoid me, Caroline?'

'Yes, I am. I don't think it's a very good idea for us to go on seeing each other.'

'You don't? But I thought we got on rather well and could have a lot of fun together.'

'I don't think your idea of fun and mine are the same.'

'I thought you liked my father, stepmother and home.'

'Yes, I do, very much indeed.'

'Well, what on earth's the trouble then?'

'The troubled is that you're only interested in me because you want to get me to bed, and once you've enjoyed me a few times, you'll just move on to the next woman that attracts you and is prepared to let you have your way with her.'

'Come on, Caroline, you can't really think that about me?'

'Yes, I can and do.'

'Well, I'm damned. I thought you liked me, and wanted me, but were just taking a bit of time to get around to it.' Billy's expression hardened. Caroline struggled to remain cool and polite.

'Oh, Billy! You're incorrigible. You must really think you're the answer to a maiden's prayer, and so you may be, but not this one's. I want more from someone than you can, or at ant rate, are prepared, to give.'

'You haven't tried me yet. You don't know what I can give, you might be surprised.'

'I think we're talking at cross purposes. I've no doubt you're very generous nor do I doubt that you're a very passionate, experienced and proficient lover. But I'm not talking about those things. I'm talking about emotional love. I'm talking about togetherness. I'm talking about knowing what the other is thinking, without a word being spoken. I'm talking about deep affection without necessarily deep penetration. I'm talking about when your partner is more important to you, than you are to yourself.'

'We haven't had a chance to get to know each other well enough for all those things yet. Let's give it a bit more time?'

'No, Billy. After last night it was quite clear to me that we're not for each other. I like you very much, but I'm not prepared to give you what you obviously want, so I think it's better that we don't see any more of each other.'

'Right, it that's the way you want it. I'll see you to your car.'

Caroline's stomach sank. She regretted her words already.

As he handed her into the limousine, he gave the driver her address.

'The car and driver have been taken care of, nothing for you to worry about. Goodbye, Caroline, take care.'

'Goodbye, Billy, and thank you for the weekend.'

As the car pulled away, Billy stood on the kerb and waved, but Caroline didn't wave back.

CHAPTER SEVEN

During Sunday night, Caroline suddenly woke up with a stifled scream as she dreamt that a plane she was flying in hit the ground in a ball of fire. It was strange how she had endured the flight with Billy with very little fear, and yet afterwards, for a couple of days, she suffered a certain amount of delayed shock. She also felt some resentment that Billy had carried on in his normal way, after the flight, without being more concerned about any possible mental reaction she might have had. This once again made her think how chauvinistic he was.

By Wednesday morning, Caroline was her old self again, and feeling somewhat surprised not to have had any calls from Billy—she knew she'd told him not to contact her—but she would have expected him to totally disregard that and call her anyway. She kept thinking about the weekend in Scotland, and in her head, hearing the sound of the pipes. Her house, which she'd always thought as quite grand, had seemed like a little hut when she'd arrived back on Sunday evening. It had been some place, the castle, and she'd liked the Grants very much. Although Elizabeth was old enough to be her mother, she seemed like a real friend, amazing after just a few days. Caroline felt she could trust Elizabeth completely and confide in her; she was also such a worldly person that there was nothing that Caroline would be embarrassed to say to her. In fact, Caroline decided, she felt much more at home with her than she did with her own mum; it made her a bit guilty thinking so, but it was true.

She brought her mind back to the job in hand, a feature she was just finishing on her experiences flying back from Scotland with Billy.

Just as she was thinking it was time for a coffee break, the phone rang. Her heart jumped, could it be Billy? She shouldn't, but she hoped it was.

'Hello,' she said.

'Is that Caroline?' asked a warm, educated, male voice.

That's not Billy, she thought. *Who on earth is it?* 'Yes, who's that?'

'It's Andrew, Andrew Campbell. How are you, Caroline?'

'Andrew, how nice of you to call. Where are you?'

'I'm in Hereford. I've just heard about your terrible flight on Sunday, and wanted to find out how you were feeling.'

'That's very nice of you. Yes, it was all rather exciting, and a bit frightening, but I'm over it all now. I must say, Billy was marvellous. I certainly wouldn't want to have an experience like that with a lesser man, or pilot, than him.'

'No, I can imagine; he's damn good in a tight spot. I only hope he was a bit sympathetic afterwards. He's a bit inclined to expect everyone to have the same steel nerves he's got. What happened about the plane, has he got it all sorted out yet?'

'I don't know, I haven't heard.'

There was a slight pause, and then Andrew asked hesitatingly, 'Hasn't he been in touch recently?'

'No, I haven't heard from him since we got back.'

'You haven't heard from him since you got back!'

'No, Andrew, Billy and I have decided not to see any more of each other.'

'Good Lord! You do surprise me; I thought it was all systems go. You seemed to be perfectly matched. Nothing to do with the trip down, was it?'

'No, nothing to do with that, I can assure you. It's just that we don't see eye to eye on one or two rather fundamental points. I think we'd better leave it at that, Andrew.'

'Ah, er, yes. I'm sorry, I didn't mean to pry, it's just that I'm so surprised, that's all. How's your diary for the rest of the week? I've got to visit a place near Northwood before the end of the week, so I thought I'd go through Oxford in the hope that we can meet. I can do it either tomorrow or Friday. I can go there very early in order to be back with you for lunch or, better still, I can visit them in the afternoon and then take you out to dinner. What do you think or are you all booked up?'

'I'd love to, it'll be so nice to see you again. Tomorrow evening would suit me fine.'

'That's really great, Caroline. Okay if I come to your house at about seven-thirty? ... Excellent, I've got your address. Looking forward to seeing you.'

Caroline sat back in her chair, it had been nice to hear Andrew's voice, and she really looked forward to seeing him again, and having a chance to talk to someone that knew the Grants so well. Perhaps she might even get some more insight into Billy—no, that was ridiculous—she already knew as much as she wanted to about him.

She made herself some coffee, and as she was going back into her study, the phone started to ring again. Damn her heart, she thought. *Why will it insist on jumping every time the phone goes?* Putting down her coffee, before her shaking hand spilt it, she picked up the phone and said, 'Hello.'

'Caroline?'

'Yes, who's that?'

'Alastair, Alastair Brown.'

'Hello, Alastair, how are you?'

'I'm fine, my dear, how are you?'

'Very well, thank you, and thank you for the cheque, which arrived on Monday.'

'Ah, you got it, good. How did you get on in Scotland?'

'I had a really super time. Lord and Lady Grant are such a nice couple. They made me feel at home from the minute I arrived to the minute I left.'

'What about Billy, did you get to know him a bit more? Are you now prepared to go to San Francisco with him looking after you?'

'No, I'd rather have someone else as my *minder*. I

don't think we two would work well together. He's a very resourceful man, and I've no doubt, very good at looking after himself, but I don't want him looking after me.'

'You do surprise me. It's not as if you're going on some package holiday together—you're not going to be in each other's pockets—but if anything should happen that needs protective action, he's the best. You must have had a few nasty minutes in that plane on Sunday evening, surely that impressed you what a good chap he is in an emergency.'

You cunning old fox, thought Caroline, *you've already been talking to Billy about all this before you called me.* 'Yes, of course, Alastair, you couldn't have a cooler, more resourceful man than Billy.'

'Well, there you are, my dear, you've answered the question yourself, Billy is the man for the job.'

'You're assuming that he still wants to do it, but you may find he's changed his mind.'

'No, I don't think he'd do that. Once Billy's said he'll do something that's it, you can rely on him one hundred per cent.'

So, thought Caroline, *you've already discussed that with him as well.* 'Perhaps nothing will come of all this business. You've not heard any more since we last talked, have you?'

'No, nothing at all. We're surprised, we'd expected an advertisement before now. It's not following the normal pattern. Anyway, Caroline, I'll be in touch as soon as I've some more news. Can I take it that you will work with Billy, when the time comes?'

'I'm not at all keen on doing so, but let's see what happens nearer the time.'

'I'm afraid that won't do, Caroline. I need to know well in advance as, if we're going to make a change, we need to start making the arrangements now. I very much want Billy to be the one to go with you as I don't think there's anyone better qualified. We were very lucky that he offered in the first place. I really do think we should be thanking him, rather than trying to get rid of him; especially when you remember that it is a job rather than a jolly.'

'Well, if I must, I suppose I must. But I would say again that I'm not very happy about it, and is that a good beginning?'

'My dear, I appreciate your agreeing, and I can assure you, you'll never regret it.'

'I just hope you're right. I certainly wouldn't want anything to go wrong.'

When they'd said goodbye to each other, Caroline

wondered to herself why she'd let him talk her into agreeing. Could it be that deep down she wanted to go with Billy? No, of course not, that was unthinkable.

Her coffee now being cold without her having drunk any of it, she decided to have a short walk, get some fresh air, and then have a light lunch out. Going to the bottom of Park Town, she was able to walk along the river for a while before cutting back to the Banbury Road, and then to the top of St Giles', and into Brown's Restaurant. Although the sun was shining, the air was much cooler, and Caroline felt really hungry after her walk, and quite ready for one of the restaurant's famous steak and Guinness pies, which, washed down with a glass of house red, made her feel at one with the world. Over coffee she sat and thought about the feature she'd just finished writing and decided to send it to the Features Editor of *Living*, as she thought it the kind of article Barbara might well buy.

As soon as she got back after lunch, she checked the answerphone. There was a message from Alastair asking her to ring him as soon as she could after three thirty. *Good old Alastair,* she thought, *out to lunch at the Savoy Grill or somewhere as luxurious, and expensive. Why did he want her to call? They'd only just spoken an hour or two ago?*

When she finally got hold of Alastair Brown, his voice

sounded more party than ever.

'Many thanks for ringing back,' he said. 'Just after we'd talked, I was informed that an advertisement has appeared in the new copy of *Kindred*. We'll have to get a letter to the advertiser as quickly as possible, which means we must meet. I can't manage tomorrow but could get you here on Friday? ... Good, then I suggest you arrive here at midday, when we can get a letter done, and afterwards go and have a spot of luncheon.'

Caroline agreed, and when she put the phone down, couldn't help laughing. That old devil, she was prepared to bet, by "hook or by crook" got himself an expenses-paid lunch every day of the week. Would Billy be there on Friday? If so, how would he behave towards her? He hadn't even tried to contact her since Sunday. He must have agreed that it was better for them not to see each other, which really wasn't very nice of him. Typical of the arrogant man he was.

In Thursday morning's post, Caroline was delighted to receive a letter from the European Editor of *Fortune* magazine telling her that they were considering printing an article on an Oxford college as it was today compared to how it would have been two hundred years ago. She was really pleased as she already had all the information she required, researched for an earlier survey she'd done for a Sunday colour supplement, the one that Lord Grant had liked so much. A phone call to the editor, with details of what she could do, and the commission was hers. She got down to it immediately, stopping only for a sandwich at lunch time, and worked on until, in late afternoon, she was interrupted by the doorbell. She wondered, *Who on earth that could be at this time of day?* Going down and opening the door, she found a delivery man standing there with a large flat cardboard box.

'Mrs Dalglish?' he asked.

'Yes, that's me.'

'Good afternoon, madame, special delivery from Episode of Knightsbridge.'

'Thanks very much,' said Caroline taking it, and wondering what it could possibly be.

When she opened the box, there was a card from Episode saying,

The enclosed suit is a replica of the one you purchased from us last Thursday; luckily, we had retained details of your measurement etc. We are also enclosing an envelope as requested by the gentleman that made the purchase. We trust it will be to your satisfaction and hope that we will have the pleasure of being of service to you in the future.

She took the suit out of the tissue paper. It was exactly like the one that had been ruined on the Sunday flight.

An envelope dropped out of it. She didn't open it immediately. She went into her bedroom and propped it up against her dressing table mirror. Then she tried on the suit. Perfect. She hung it up in her wardrobe, put on a negligee, picked up the letter, and sat down in her bedroom armchair.

She just looked at the envelope for a few minutes wondering what Billy was going to say in it. Well, it'd got to be from Billy, hadn't it? She laughed aloud. There wasn't anyone else who'd send it, was there? She turned the envelope, letting her long fingers caress it, then she slid her finger under the flap and gently opened it. There was a single sheet of paper inside. She unfolded it and looked at the bold handwriting. It was the first time she'd seen anything written by Billy.

She read:

Caroline,

I'm sorry about what happened on Sunday, it was just one of those things. In all my years of flying I've never been struck by lightning before, and very much doubt if I ever will be again.

I must congratulate you on the way you handled yourself during the emergency, first-class, just as good as one of my boys.

I realised that the very smart new suit you were wearing was completely ruined by the rain and muck from the side of the plane as we made an emergency disembarkation so, as I was lucky enough to know where you purchased it, I've been able to replace it. Trust all goes well with you.

Billy.

Caroline held the letter in her hand and looked into space. It was what she should have expected him to say, but not what she'd hoped for! It was so unfriendly. It said what it had to, and nothing more. It had the feel of a letter from the commanding officer to one of his men. It wasn't the letter from someone that found you attractive and wanted to be with you.

'Come on, Caroline, come on,' she said out loud. *You know exactly what he wants,* she thought, *and it's to do with wanting all right, but nothing to do with wanting to be with.* She must stop all this daydreaming. It was already past six, and Andrew would be here at seven-thirty.

She ought to thank Billy. She phoned his office to be

told he was out and not expected back until the morning. She tried his home number. There was no reply. Her mouth felt dry and she could feel her heart beating. This was ridiculous, she thought, all this just because she might have had to speak to him.

By the time Andrew rang the front doorbell at seven-thirty, Caroline was ready. She was dressed in the Louis Feraud suit that she'd bought for Scotland, but had never worn. Opening the door, she was struck again by what an attractive man Andrew was.

'Hello, Caroline,' he said, holding out a lovely bouquet of yellow roses. 'You look even more beautiful that I'd remembered.'

'Thank you, and what lovely flowers. You'll come in and have a drink?'

'Yes, please.'

When they'd got a drink and were sitting down, Andrew said, 'This is a jolly attractive house, Caroline, and very conveniently placed. I've booked a table at Weston Manor for eight-thirty. I hope that suits.'

'Yes, that'll be fun. I haven't been there for ages. It's so nice to see you again Andrew, and quite unexpected.'

'Well, I enjoyed meeting you at the Grants', and wanted the chance of having you to myself for an evening.

This seemed like the perfect opportunity. Have you heard anything from any of them since the weekend?'

'Only a present from Billy that arrived a few hours ago. He sent me a suit to replace the one that got written-off during all the drama on Sunday evening. It was very kind of him, but quite unnecessary. It wasn't his fault. It was just one of those things.'

'That was very considerate of him, but I'm surprised he sent it rather than bringing it personally.'

'It's as I mentioned on the phone, we've decided not to fraternise anymore.'

'I'm amazed. Not just because you seem to be so suited to each other, but also because you seem to have parted almost before you even met. If I've got it right, you only met about a week ago, and as you decided not to see any more of each other as from last Sunday, the whole thing lasted five or six days.'

'Perhaps it's not so surprising if you know the whole story. Do you, for instance, know how we first met a few months ago? No ... well.' And Caroline told him about the embassy meeting. She was surprised that she was now able to laugh about it herself. Andrew, of course, thought it very funny.

'Trust old Billy to get someone like you to have to

frisk. If it happens to me, you can guarantee it's always an enormously fat, ugly woman with a disagreeable smell. That didn't put you off him though, after all, he was only doing his job, wasn't he?'

'Yes, I see it like that now but at the time I was furious. He was so nonchalant and didn't say sorry. In fact, he actually told me off and said I was lucky it hadn't been worse. He really is very arrogant.'

'I wouldn't disagree with that. He's always been. We've been friends almost since we were born. Billy's a couple of years older than me, and he's always been the same. His main problem is he just doesn't trust women. Not his fault really. You've heard what happened about his mother leaving?'

Here we go again, thought Caroline, *everyone makes excuses for him, and anything he does wrong is not his fault but because of what his poor old mum did twenty-five years ago.* 'Yes, I know all about that, but he's a big boy now and should have got over it by this time. I think he just hides behind it as he really doesn't want to get close to a woman.'

'You may have something there, it could be true, but I don't think so. He's like most tough guys. He needs someone who can give him love and affection.'

'I bet he gets plenty of physical love.'

'Yes, I'm sure he does, but not the love and affection he needs, because he finds it impossible to be trusting enough to recognise it when it's there. I think it's time we went, Caroline, if you're ready.'

As the car approached Weston Manor Hotel, Andrew said, 'Billy and I used to come here a lot at one time, when we were at Hereford together. He had a girlfriend living in the village and I'd got one who lived just down the road at Islip. We had a lot of fun here. It's very nice, particularly in summer with its swimming pool and gardens.'

They didn't go into the bar but straight into the panelled dining room where they sipped an aperitif while they studied the menu.

Caroline decided she really liked Andrew as they chatted over their starters. He was so relaxed and seemed gentle compared to Billy.

As the plates were being cleared after their delicious main course, there was a sudden change in the atmosphere in the room, which had been so quiet and subdued. It wasn't that there was a great deal of noise or anything like that, but the waiters were all smiling, and moving towards the other end of the room, and there was almost a feeling of general anticipation. Caroline thought there must be a pop star or member of royalty about to arrive, but as she was facing the wrong way, she couldn't see who came in, and was left in suspense until Andrew said, 'Oh my God! Billy!'

Caroline couldn't resist turning her head to get a better look, and there he was, surrounded by fawning staff as he held the chair for his stunning companion to sit down. And stunning she was, titian hair cascading over her almost bare shoulders, voluptuous breasts hardly hidden by her halter-necked décolleté dress, and a face that seemed too perfect to be true. Caroline turned back and gulped in life-saving oxygen. This was too much.

'I'm sorry, Caroline, I never thought for a moment he'd be here. I didn't even realise that he was still seeing Stephanie.'

At that moment, Billy suddenly saw Andrew and came across the restaurant to their table. As he was saying hello, he suddenly saw that it was Caroline with Andrew. He looked quite annoyed and said, 'What are you two doing here together?'

'The same as you, chum, having dinner,' said Andrew, obviously not too pleased by Billy's tone.

'Why don't you go and say hello to Stephanie while I have a quick word with Caroline?'

Andrew looked at Caroline with a raised eyebrow, she

responded with an almost indiscernible nod.

'Okay, Billy, but we're in the middle of our meal so we won't make it long, will we?'

As Andrew went across the room, Billy perched on his chair and, glaring at Caroline, asked abruptly, 'What are you doing here with Andrew?'

'I would have thought that fairly obvious, Billy, having dinner.'

'Is that all?'

'What else is there? I'm certainly not doing a cabaret turn or anything.'

'No, you know what I mean ... afterwards.'

'After dinner Andrew will take me home, and I'm sure he'll not try and force me to do anything I don't want to, as some others seem to delight in doing, in their heavy-handed, boorish way.'

'Are you telling me the truth?'

'Let's get this straight. It's no concern of yours what I decide to do. Hadn't you better get back to your seductress or she may have smouldered right away?'

'I introduced you to Andrew, so I feel it is my concern.'

'Please go away, Billy, and let me and Andrew continue with, what had been, until now, a very pleasant evening.'

As Andrew came back to their table, Billy went off

across the room without another word.

Caroline was livid. She didn't know when she'd been more annoyed. She felt quite ill for a moment with a mixture of pent-up emotions.

'I'm sorry about that, that's not at all like Billy. He's usually so cool, calm and collected. He wasn't actually rude to you, was he?'

'Yes, he was, he had the cheek to ask what we were doing here together. What it's got to do with him I don't know. It's not as if he and I are anything to each other.'

'I think you must have that wrong. Maybe he's nothing to you, but you must be something to him. There's no other explanation for his bad-mannered behaviour. It's just not like Billy. He may be arrogant and everything but that was just not him.'

'I've just thought, how awful of me, I didn't say anything about the suit he sent me.'

'Don't worry, we can pause at his table on the way out.'

'I'm not too sure that's a good idea,' Caroline said with a nervous laugh.

'He can't be that bad, he's got to have cooled down before we leave. Mind you, I wasn't too pleased with the way he spoke to me either. Lucky girl Stephanie, she's going to have a bit of a bad-tempered companion this evening, unless I'm very mistaken.'

They both laughed and Caroline began to feel a little more human again.

'Who is Stephanie, I take it she's the one who lives in this village?'

'Yes, at least this is her home base, but she's all over the world. You must have seen her face on the front of things like *Vogue*. She's a very, very top model.'

'Yes, of course. Now I know who she is—Stephanie Thompson. I'd have recognised her, but I only got a blurred impression. Although with her even that should have been enough. In fact, I did meet her once, for a few minutes, when I was doing a feature for *Company* magazine on top-earning models. Quite a girl I remember, and earning so much money it made the mind boggle.'

'Yes, that's her. Surprisingly, under it all she's rather a nice girl. She's very fond of Billy but he only looks on her as a "friend". I'm sorry she wastes her time on him. He'll never be serious where she's concerned.'

'You don't think so?'

'No, he might have done once. They were pretty close for the best part of a year, and then Billy had to go away for a few months—he was still serving then—and they promised to be true to each other until he got back.

After three or four months, Stephanie, who is very warm-blooded, just had to have a man in her bed or die. She only did it for the physical side, and still wanted Billy more than anything, or anyone, else. He found out, but took it much more calmly that any of us would have believed, which only proved she hadn't meant all that much to him after all. But, as you can guess, it just proved to him, once again, that women were not to be trusted. Surprisingly, they still have a good friendship going, based on their mutual admiration for each other in bed.'

'Being a man you wouldn't agree with me, but the more I hear about Billy, the more I think he's like an old-fashioned, chauvinistic pirate.'

Andrew roared with laughter. He loved it. 'I wish some of his old mates could hear you say that, and there are a couple of generals who'd enjoy it too.' He went on chuckling away as they finished their coffee.

As they made their way across the room after dinner, Caroline could see Billy and Stephanie sitting at their table. As they reached the table, Billy stood up and introduced Caroline and Stephanie. Caroline had to admit to herself that the other girl had fabulous good looks and she was afraid she must look very "plain Jane" beside her.

'I know your work, Caroline. I enjoy it very much; you're a very good writer.'

'Thank you, and I know your face. I always thought it must be the camera that made you look quite so beautiful, but now I know it's not, the camera doesn't lie.'

'That's very nice of you. We met once, didn't we?'

'Yes, I did an article which you featured in.'

'Of course, I remember.'

'Well, if you two girls have finished complimenting each other, why don't you and Andrew join us for a drink?'

'That's kind of you, Billy, but I'd like to get home now, and I'm sure Andrew will want to start back on his journey. I did try and ring you today, Billy, to thank you for your very kind present. It was quite unnecessary as the damage was no fault of yours. It was just one of those things.'

'That's okay. I felt responsible and only hope you didn't find the experience too shocking.'

Caroline and Andrew said their goodbyes and left the hotel.

When they got back to Park Town, Andrew accepted an offer to have a quick cup of coffee before starting on his journey. They sat in the kitchen, on either side of the large pine table, sipping their coffee.

'I really do think that you and Billy could get together. He's such an old friend there's nothing I'd rather see than him with someone as beautiful, intelligent and sincere as you.'

'Andrew, you mustn't flatter me so much. It'll go to my head and I'll get a false, inflated opinion of myself. You might like the idea of Billy and me together, but I don't think I can imagine anything worse. Don't get me wrong, I think him very handsome, very attractive, very sexy and I find he excites me more than any other man I've ever known. But how could I have any kind of relationship with a man who didn't think he could depend on me? How could I have a relationship with any man that treats me as though I'm one of his goods and chattels? No, Andrew, unfortunately, I don't think Billy and I are for each other.'

Alastair was very welcoming when Caroline arrived at his office on Friday. He poured her some coffee and then showed her the advertisement that they were going to answer. There was a heading—*Foundation of the Divine Spirit*—then it simply said:

[If your inner life is empty, you need to join us when, together with other soulmates, you will find a new meaning to, and understanding of, life; through this your personal fulfilment will soar to unbelievable levels. Membership of our sect is only open to those that meet our stringent personal requirements; don't waste any more precious time, write now for an interview to find out how you can lead a better, more fulfilled life.]

Then there was a box number, etc.

'Surely people don't really fall for that sort of thing, do they, Alastair?'

'Good Lord, my dear, you'd be surprised how gullible a great many people are. This cult business is big. There are four or five hundred in this country alone, and they use deceptive and psychologically manipulative techniques to recruit the unsuspecting; one of which you're about to become.'

They laughed together, but Caroline began to wonder if it really was a matter for laughing or not.

They drafted a short letter just saying that she was a young widow looking for something more to her life. Alastair also managed, in a subtle way, to give the impression that she was not short of money.

'There we are,' he said, 'that should do the job.' His internal phone rang. 'Yes, show him in please ... Billy's arrived. I thought it would be nice if he joined us for luncheon.'

'He didn't mention it when I bumped into him yesterday evening.'

'I only asked him this morning ... Morning, Billy, come

on in. We've just devised a letter to our friends. Here, read it, and see what you think.'

'Hello, Caroline, how are you?'

'I'm fine thanks. See what you think of the letter.'

'Yes ... um ... yes. Very good, just the right touch. I'm sure they'll ask you to go and see them when they've read that.'

'Good,' said Alastair. 'I'm glad you approve. Are you both ready for some lunch? Good, let's go then.'

Caroline was glad that they were not going to sit in Alastair's office talking, as the arrival of Billy had had that funny effect on her again. Her mouth had dried up and her face felt all taught—almost as though she was wearing a mask. When she smiled, she thought she must look very false and strange, though by the way Billy was looking at her he didn't seem to have noticed anything odd.

When they got into Alastair's large, black, official car, Caroline ended up on the back seat between the two men. There should have been plenty of room for the three of them, but Billy's body was hard against Caroline's, so she moved a little towards Alastair, but it didn't seem to make any difference, so she moved a little further.

Alastair, who must have felt her body beginning to

press against his, asked, 'Are you comfortable?'

'Yes thanks, Alastair,' she said, but Billy was still pressed against her. Why was it he always felt so warm? It was more than just feeling warm. It was almost as though he actually generated extra heat. *God,* she thought, *his body does feel good!*

The two men chatted over her head until they reached the restaurant where they were lunching: *Le Pont de la Tour.*

'This place has only been open a few weeks, and it's the first time I've been. I've been told it's very good, which I hope is correct.'

Caroline wondered if she was going to be able to eat anything. Sitting squashed up to Billy had made her feel quite heady and, almost, slightly sick. *My God,* she thought, *I'm just like some inexperienced teenage girl when she meets some pop star idol. This is ridiculous.*

The restaurant was long, narrow and luxurious. As they entered and Alastair was asking about his table, the head waiter came up and, bowing, said, 'Good afternoon, Mr Grant, how nice to see you again.'

Here we go again, thought Caroline. *Is there anywhere he's not known?*

After they'd ordered their food and were enjoying an

aperitif, Alastair said, 'It looks as though things could start to happen, at long last. We should get a reply to our letter within a few days, and your meeting, Caroline, within a few days of that.'

'I shall be glad when something starts happening,' she replied, 'as, although it's under two weeks since all this started, it seems to have been going on for ages.'

'Yes, my dear, I agree. What's the matter with you, Billy, you don't look your usual happy self?'

'Well, I'm still not at all sure we should be getting Caroline into this business. It might turn out to be very distressing, or even dangerous for her. After all, it's not the sort of thing she's experienced in.'

'My dear Billy, surely you're not going over all that again. Caroline has made her mind up. There's no need for you to go on clucking like an old hen over its chicks. As to experience, if she could do that Afghanistan thing, I'm sure this will be child's play to her.'

'What Afghanistan thing?'

Caroline felt that, for the moment, they'd both forgotten her presence.

'Do you mean, Billy, that you didn't read that brilliant piece by her when she went out and lived, for several weeks, with the Mujahideen fighting the Russian occupation forces, and wrote a profile of their leader? It was acclaimed by everyone. I made a note of her name at that time as someone who might be able to help me at a future date. You do surprise me, I thought you knew all that, and knew that's why I'd chosen her for this little escapade.'

Billy sat for a minute looking into space, and then, as if he suddenly remembered that she was there, turned to Caroline and said, in a slightly accusing voice, 'You never told me about that, Caroline.'

'I'm sorry, Billy,' she answered with an edge to her voice. 'I didn't know you wanted a list of everything I've written in the last two years.'

'What with that, and a father that was an SOE war hero, I'm beginning to get the feeling that you've not told me very much about yourself.'

'What do you mean SOE hero?' broke in Alastair.

'Well, that cheers me up no end. Don't tell me I know something you don't about Caroline?' Billy laughed, his usual good humour returning at last. 'Caroline's maiden name was Johnson and her father is George Johnson.'

'What, George Johnson of the French Resistance?'

'None other.'

'I don't believe it, not George, I knew him so well. Caroline, I lost touch with him after we all tried, including

Billy's father, to get him some further recognition. But he just wanted to lead a quiet family life and to left in peace. What's the latest news about him, how is he, what's he doing now?'

Caroline gave him a brief rundown on what her father had done with his life, and how he, and her mother, were now living in a Cornish cottage, in retirement. She was quite touched by the interest, and obvious respect, that Alastair showed in him.

When they got back to Alastair's office after lunch, Caroline asked him if she could tell her parents about San Francisco, and he agreed as long as it was only them.

Caroline was then ready to go and catch a train back to Oxford, but Billy, as she'd expected, invited her to stay on in London and have dinner with him, but he explained that he would have to leave her on her own for the afternoon, as he had things he had to do. This gave Caroline the chance to decline, which, as soon as she had, she regretted, realising that she'd only done it "on principle". He didn't give her the chance to change her mind as he didn't repeat the invitation. She felt quite put out by his not trying to persuade her.

'Okay,' he said, 'in that case let me send you back with one of the boys.'

'That won't be necessary, I can quite easily go back by train.'

'Wouldn't hear of it. I'll just phone for someone.'

A few minutes later, they were told the car had arrived, and when they reached reception, there was Fred waiting for them, with a big grin on his face. As she turned to say goodbye to Billy, he looked into her eyes and said, 'I'm sorry you don't want to stay in town for dinner, and the spend the night with me. I just don't know why we can't hit it off, I don't think I've done anything to offend you.'

'That's the answer, Billy, you don't even know what's wrong with your behaviour and general manner. I could like you a lot, but not while you behave towards me in the way you do.'

He was just about to reply when the girl in reception interrupted, calling out, 'There's an urgent call for you, Mr Grant. Will you take it here or would you like to go into one of the offices?'

Looking at Caroline, he said, 'Hell, I'll have to take it. I'll phone you. Take care.'

Caroline had her usual amusing conversation with Fred, who now looked upon her as a long-established friend. He gladly accepted her offer of a cup of tea when they got back to her Park Town house, and by the time he left it was already nearly half-past six. Caroline went into her study and turned on the answer phone. The first message was from Andrew.

'Hello, Caroline, this is Andrew, Andrew Campbell. Sorry I've missed you, but I just wanted to say how much I enjoyed seeing you last night. We must get together again soon, very soon. I'll try you again, maybe later today, or any way, tomorrow.'

Caroline thought once again what a nice voice Andrew had and what a super person he was. If nothing else came of knowing Billy, she would at least have made one good friend through him. The second call was from her daily, who said, 'Hello, Mrs Dalglish. I'm better now. I'll be in to clean you up Monday.'

Caroline laughed. *Talking of being cleaned up,* she thought, *a Scotch and a nice hot bath wouldn't be a bad idea.* But before she could leave her study, the phone rang. It was Billy's mellow, and decidedly sexy, voice at the other end.

'Caroline, I'm sorry I didn't have much of a chance to talk to you today as there were quite a few things I wanted to say, and now I've got to dash off to Geneva, and won't be back until late on Sunday. I just wish we could get things sorted out between us. I think all our problems are because of our first meeting in the embassy.'

'No, I don't think so, Billy. I've forgiven, and almost forgotten, about that now. It's other things.'

'I can't think what those can be, but the telephone's not the place to discuss them. We'll have to wait until I get back. I'll call you on my return so that we can meet.'

'Yes, all right, I'll wait to hear from you.'

'Great. I've just been talking to Elizabeth, and she was saying how much she and Dad liked you and enjoyed having you for the weekend. She also said what a nice thank-you letter she'd received from you. The long and the short of it is that they want us to go up and stay, to attend a charity ball, that is to be held in the castle. The ball's on Saturday, the thirty-first of October, and they'd like us to go up as long before it as possible, and certainly not later than the previous Thursday, and to stay on after it until the following weekend. Elizabeth is writing to you about it all and sending you an official invitation. What do you think, it should be great fun, shouldn't it?'

Caroline held her breath for a moment, what a wonderful invitation, to spend ten days or so with Billy, and the Grants, and to be a guest of theirs at a ball in their castle. What a dream, but how could she go with the situation as it was with Billy only interested in getting her into bed to satisfy his lust.

'Are you still there, Caroline?'

'Yes, I'm sorry, Billy, I was thinking. The first point is, don't you think we may well be in San Francisco at that time? Secondly, I'm not sure that, in any case, I'd want to go with you.'

'You must be mad. There are at least a dozen girls I know that would give their eye teeth to go to the ball with me.'

'Then I suggest you take one of them,' Caroline said as she slammed the phone down.

To start with, her reaction was pure rage that he should say such a thing to her, then it turned to, almost, despair. They would never get together. They would never understand each other. He was the most charismatic man she'd ever met. If she just wanted someone for a short affair, he'd be perfect, but that was not what she wanted, that was not her style. She'd just have to forget Billy and find someone else. But there just wasn't anyone else she'd ever met who could hold a candle to him. Oh God, what a mess. She'd found a nearly perfect man, but it was just not to be.

She just didn't want any more calls, at the moment,

so she set the answer phone and went and lay in a hot, perfumed bath. After her bath she felt a little better, and putting on a negligee, went into the drawing room and poured herself a Scotch. She sat for a while, in a half-trance, wondering what was going to happen to her life. One thing she must do was to ring her parents and arrange to go and see them before she went to San Francisco. Going into the kitchen, she made herself a sandwich and took it up to her study. The answer phone eye was flashing so she turned it on to see who had called. It was Billy's voice.

'I tried you again immediately after your line went dead but only got this machine. I'm sorry if what I said offended you. I'll call you as soon as I'm back from Geneva. Have a nice weekend and try and think nice things about me.'

Well, at least he'd said he was sorry. Caroline was surprised, she'd thought that probably he didn't even know how to say the word!

She nibbled her sandwiches and then dialled her parents' number. Her mother answered. After the usual exchange of information on how they all were and what they had been doing, Caroline said, 'I'd like to come down and see you sometime next week. Are you going to be around?'

'Yes, dear, a fairly clear week, I think. How long will you stay for?'

'I might just come for the day. I've got rather a lot on.'

'That's going to be rather a heavy day for you, and we'd much rather you stayed for a while. Are you sure you can't?'

'I'd love to stay, Mum, but I just don't think it's possible at the moment.'

'Obviously, we'd rather have you down for the day than nothing at all, but see what you can do, perhaps you can squeeze just one night in.'

'I'll try, Mum. Is Dad there?'

'No, he's just gone out with the old dog. Did you want him for something?'

'No, nothing in particular. I just wanted to tell him off for never having told me he was a war hero.'

'He never tells anyone about that. He wants to forget it all.'

'Tell him I've heard all about his exploits from Lord Grant. I stayed with Lord and Lady Grant at their castle in Scotland, and he sent his very best wishes to Dad and said he'd like you both to go and stay when you're next up that way.'

'That was very nice of him, but I can't see us getting

up to Scotland again.'

'Perhaps we could all go together sometime?'

'That would be lovely, darling.'

After talking to her mother, Caroline felt in a much better frame of mind and, to her surprise, had a really good night's sleep.

It was a quiet, uneventful weekend, except for Sunday when Andrew drove to Oxford and took her out to lunch in Woodstock. He didn't stay long as he was getting ready to go away, on something or other, that he wasn't allowed to say anything about. *These army types,* thought Caroline, *seem to love all this "cloak and dagger" stuff.* But there was no denying that Andrew was an extremely likeable person.

Monday morning, things started with a bang. Alastair rang at eight-thirty to say that a letter had arrived from the *Foundation of the Divine Spirit* asking her to phone them. He gave her their phone number and asked her to call them and make an appointment for the earliest possible date. She phoned them just after nine, and spoke to a rather smarmy-sounding man. They agreed that she'd go to their premises, in the Upper Richmond Road in London, at ten o'clock the next morning. She then spoke to Alastair again, who said that a car would pick her up at eight-thirty and take her to the interview.

Shortly after that call, the phone went again, and it was Billy.

'Hello, Caroline. I've only just flown in from Geneva. I couldn't get back last night after all. How's everything? Did you have a nice weekend?'

'Yes, thanks, Billy. You've not spoken to Alastair yet? … No, well, we've heard from our friends, and I've a meeting at ten in the morning, at their place in Richmond.'

'I'll talk to him and come straight back to you.'

Ten minutes later he was back on the phone again.

'That's all fixed, Caroline. I'll pick you up about eight-thirty and take you there. We can discuss details during the drive. May I suggest that you dress in something expensive but subdued. Don't forget that your part is a well-off, slightly mousy, lonely widow interested in things to with the occult, mysticism, good works and everything "green". You'll have to try to tone yourself down a bit as it wouldn't be right for you to arrive looking your normal divine, delicious and fantastically desirable self.'

Caroline had to laugh. 'Billy, you really are, as always, quite incorrigible. Anyway, I'll do as you suggest, and I'll make sure I'm ready by eight-thirty.'

'Great. Alastair says he wants us to go back there as soon as you've finished your interview. So, if it's okay with you, I'll drive you back to Oxford afterwards, and perhaps we can have a bit of time to talk together?'

'That sounds like a good idea as, as soon as the various arrangements are made, I've got to go down to Cornwall for at least a day.'

'To see your parents?'

'That's right.'

'If you're going down and back in the same day, could I drive you? I'd enjoy having the day with you, and I'd also like to meet your father, and of course, your mother.'

'I don't know, Billy, let's talk about it when we see each other tomorrow.'

'Yes fine. What are you doing today, anything?'

'Yes, stacks of work. I've got a lot I must get done in case I have to suddenly go away.'

'Same as me. Seen any more of old Andrew since the other night?'

'Only on Sunday. He took me to lunch.'

'Nice chap, Andrew, don't you think?'

Yes, and I know what you're thinking, thought Caroline, grinning to herself. 'Yes, I agree, I think he's an absolute sweetie, one of the nicest men I've met for a long time, and such good fun to be with.'

'Oh, yes … er … um … quite. Seeing him again soon?'

'No, unfortunately he's got to go away on some army thing and doesn't even know when he'll be back.'

'That's the trouble with having a friend in the services, particularly the SAS, you just never know when they're going to disappear for weeks on end.'

Caroline was now near to laughter. Billy hadn't the faintest idea she was ribbing him. He was being absurdly transparent. Perhaps he did feel a bit more for her than just lust.

'Billy, I must go, my daily has just arrived. See you tomorrow.'

By quarter past eight on Tuesday morning, Caroline was ready to go. She was wearing the dark grey suit that she'd worn at John's memorial service and hadn't got rid of for sentimental reasons. Although of top quality, it was very strait-laced and looking a bit old-fashioned. She had tied her hair back in a tight ponytail, leaving her ears sticking out, then she pulled on a blue beret so that it almost covered the rest of her golden hair. She didn't put on any make-up or any of her usual perfume.

Looking in the mirror she was pleased, and amazed, at how different she looked to her normal self; a relatively few changes and she looked positively dull. She hoped it wouldn't put Billy off, or did she? Yes, she decided that she definitely did. *Oh my God,* she thought, *I still seem to change my mind every few hours, or even minutes.*

There was a ring at the door and, opening it, she found a smiling Billy. He looked at her for a minute and then he laughed loudly. 'I wouldn't have believed it. You look absolutely different. If I'd met you in the street, I'd not have recognised you; you've done a brilliant job. You look just right.' He leant forward and kissed her gingerly on the cheek. She wasn't sure whether this was because he was uncertain of his reception, or because the way she looked he didn't fancy anything more familiar.

She felt excited, very excited. There were collywobbles in her stomach. It was not just that her escapade into the unknown was about to start. Even more than that, it was seeing Billy again.

As they left the house, she looked for his Porsche, not there. She looked for the black Range Rover, not there. The only vehicle standing outside her house was a somewhat scruffy looking London taxi. As Billy took her arm and led her towards it, Fred's head came out of the driver's compartment. 'Good morning, Mrs D. Didn't know I'm a taxi driver in my spare time, did you?' he said, followed by a loud guffaw.

'This is just one of the undercover vehicles that we

sometimes use. Fred doesn't normally drive it, but when he heard you were involved, I couldn't stop him.'

'Well, got to look after you Mrs D, 'aven't I?'

'Yes, Fred, and very well you do too.'

'Now you two, if you can cut the social chatter, perhaps I can talk for a minute about this morning's job. Don't forget, Caroline, that you're meant to be arriving from central London, hence the taxi. Fred will drop me before we arrive at the house and then take you to the front door. He'll wait there for you to come out, and this is where we have to be a little careful. If they're real professionals they're going to notice, and be suspicious, that he's waiting for you. It's unusual for a taxi to wait, but you'll just have to say that as you didn't expect to be there long, he'd agreed to hang on. Hopefully they won't even notice. If, however, they tell you to let him go and that they'll get you another taxi or give you a lift when you're ready to leave, agree. If that happens, don't worry about it, we'll be watching the house, and ready to follow if necessary. I don't think anything like that will happen, but we just want to be ready for anything. Anyway, this must all seem very mundane to someone that ran around with the Mujahideen.'

'Were you with the Mujahideen, Mrs D?' asked Fred

with a definite air of respect.

'Yes, she was Fred, but this is not the time to discuss it. Will you kindly concentrate on your appalling driving and not keep interrupting.'

'Sorry for living, boss.'

It didn't take long to reach Putney, as this was something more than just an old taxi.

'Billy, isn't the house in Richmond?'

'No, it's in the Upper Richmond Road, and just in Putney. You've got the number, Fred, let's find it, and drive past so that we can assess the situation. There it is, that grey Victorian house with the Jag in the drive. It's perfect, when you take her back, Fred, you can park outside in the road, and with that bit of hedge, I don't think they'll even see you. Caroline, there's only one more point and that's money. They may ask you for some sort of subscription or contribution, so Alastair has had an account opened in your name at Barclays, Kensington, where he has deposited five thousand pounds. Here's a cheque book, personalised for you, so if you feel you have to give them something, just go ahead.'

Fred couldn't resist butting in with his little comment. 'Cor, that sounds a bit of all right. We could nip off to Paris together on that, Mrs D.'

'Is that a definite proposition, Fred?'

'For God's sake, Caroline, don't you start as well. Fred's quite enough on his own without any help from you. I'm trying to run a serious operation here and not a day out for budding comics.'

Fred turned right round and gave her a big wink, but Caroline resisted saying any more as she realised that Billy was getting a bit nervous on her behalf. Taking his hand, she squeezed it, and looking at him, smiled and said, 'I'll be okay. I'll just do exactly what you've told me to.'

Still holding her hand, he smiled back, his eyes holding hers, and he said softly, 'You make sure you take care. I don't want anything happening to you.'

It was silly, but Caroline felt closer to him then, than perhaps at any time before. She just wanted to hold him and be with him.

'You'd better get out here, boss,' interrupted Fred. 'That's a good place for you to wait, in the entrance to that block of flats. You'll be able to watch the house from there without being obvious.'

'Yes, good thinking, Fred.' His hand was still holding hers. As Caroline was on the pavement side of the cab, Billy had to pass in front of her to get out. As he did so, he leant forward and kissed her on the lips. 'Good luck, and be careful,' he said as he got out onto the pavement. She looked back and she saw him enter the doorway of the block of flats.

'Here we are, Mrs D. Now, mind how you go, and don't forget "the cavalry" are outside if you need us.'

'Thanks, Fred, see you soon.'

She walked back to the gate and up the short drive to the front door, where she rang the bell. After a few minutes, the door was opened by a thin, tallish man who she'd guess was in his late thirties. He gave the impression of being colourless. Everything about him was nondescript, and the eyes that looked at her, from under his almost non-existent eyebrows, were cold and humourless. There was something actually unpleasant about him; he sent a little shiver up her spine.

'Mrs Dalglish? Come in.'

The entrance hall had a mosaic floor and a cold atmosphere. The man opened a door leading off the hall and stood aside for her to enter the room beyond. It was a well-proportioned room, and comfortably furnished, with sofas and chairs in faded chintz.

'Do sit down. Will you have a cup of coffee? Just a minute, I'll organise it.'

He went out and Caroline could hear him calling to

someone, then he was back again.

'I'm sorry,' said Caroline, 'I'm not sure of your name.'

'I'm Charles. I'm not usually here, I'm just standing in for Robert who's away at the moment. We had your letter about your interest in us. We in turn are interested in you.'

He then went into a long spiel about mystical powers and how any member would need to have religious faith in their guru; how they believed in frugality and shared their minds and possessions with the needy.

He then asked her, 'Does your present religion fulfil your spiritual needs?'

What was she meant to answer to that?

'No, not completely.'

'Are you looking for more spiritual fulfilment?'

'Yes, most certainly.'

'Do you live with or are you in close touch with your parents and or other relations or friends?'

Better not to be, she thought. 'No, I've no parents or close relations now.'

'Are you interested in meeting people of a similar type to yourself?'

'Yes, very much.'

'Are you interested in helping humanity?'

'Yes, in whatever small way I can.'

'Do you have much spare time, or are you in the position that you have to spend the greatest percentage of your time working?'

'I can take whatever time I need.'

'May I ask if this means you have enough money of your own not to have to bother about working?'

'More or less.'

'If you wanted to be part of our sect, you'd have to go to our foundation head in San Francisco to learn about our way of life, and how we can make you into a whole new person. This will incur you an expense. We give all our money and worldly possessions to help the needy, so we can't assist in cost of this nature. You'd have to pay your own fares, but we would accommodate you in the building where we have our shrine. Is any of this a problem to you?'

'No, none at all,' said Caroline, wondering who paid for the Jag standing in the driveway.

'We always ask anyone joining us to make a contribution towards our running costs. Would you be prepared to do that?'

'Yes, but what sort of amount are you suggesting, and when would you want it?'

'People give what they like as a first contribution,

some give ten, twenty or thirty thousand, but we do have a minimum of one thousand pounds. If you are really interested in make a new life for yourself, and in joining a large circle of like-minded friends, of both sexes, then make your initial contribution as quickly as you can so that I can put all the arrangements in hand.'

'Well, I could give you a cheque for a thousand pounds now, if that's all right?'

'Yes, that'll be adequate for now.' After she'd given him the cheque, he said, 'I'll send on all the details of when and where within the next day or two. Can you be ready to go at short notice?'

'Within a few days of hearing from you.'

'Fine. Thank you for coming. I'll be in touch.'

He saw her to the door and that was that. *What a creep,* she thought. If she'd been there under her own steam, she'd have told him a thing or two. She didn't even get that cup of coffee.

As soon as she got in the *taxi,* Fred drove back to the flats, and parked round the far corner. 'Just in case anyone's watching.'

When Billy got in, he looked very pleased, and relieved, to see her. 'How did you get on? You were very quick.'

'Long enough for him to take a thousand pounds of

Alastair's money.' Then she described "Charles" and all that had happened. 'I must say, Billy, if that's the way they carry on, I'm surprised they get anyone to join.'

'There are an awful lot of very lonely people just looking for *friends*, and something to interest them. I don't expect they have any problems finding enough willing victims. You can see from your own experience they don't consider that they've got to take a lot of trouble with people.'

'Reckon I'm in the wrong business, boss. Where to?'

'Back to Sir Alastair's please, Fred.'

Alastair Brown, as expected, took them out to lunch where they discussed what had happened at Caroline's morning meeting.

At the end of the discussion Alastair turned to Caroline and asked, 'What do you think, Caroline? You're a trained observer and interviewer, what is your impression of these people, and what do you think they're up to?'

'In my opinion, from what I've heard and seen to date, they're not part of a drugs ring. I think they're getting hold of well-off, lonely or disturbed people, and fleecing them. He talked this morning of every member having a personal spiritual adviser. This wouldn't be necessary, or practical, if this was to do with smuggling. I feel drugs may well come into it from the other angle, that is if they can get people hooked, it'll be easier to part them from their money.'

'Good, yes. What's your opinion, Billy?'

'I go along with Caroline.'

'I feel that you're right, but what about the two girls who disappeared?'

'A coincidence, nothing to do directly with the Foundation. Do you agree, Billy?'

Billy nodded and Alastair said, 'We'll have to carry on, the Foreign Office will want more information than we've got. As soon as you hear about San Francisco, you'd better get out there, and get the job done. Billy, you carry on as before. Don't let anything slip and treat it as if we expect the worst. We don't want any accidents.'

CHAPTER NINE

As Caroline and Billy swooshed down the motorway in Billy's Porsche, Caroline was able to relax and to think about the previous day. It had been quite a day. What with the meeting in the morning with the Foundation, and then her evening with Billy, a lot to think about. When they'd left Alastair, Billy had been sweet and she really began to think that perhaps things might lead to, if nothing else, a lasting friendship. They'd got back to Oxford in time for a late cup of tea, and after a bit of general chatter, she'd asked him if he'd like to have a spot of supper at the house. He'd agreed with alacrity but said, as they'd had one of Alastair's enormous luncheons, not to bother with anything fancy.

That suited her fine as she knew she'd got plenty of

smoked salmon, salads, cheese and French bread. She'd gone into the kitchen to prepare a few things, and to get out from the fridge the bottle of champagne that she just happened to have popped in there before she left that morning. Then she'd shown Billy where the downstairs cloakroom was and went upstairs to have a quick shower and to change out of her Foundation get-up. When she'd showered and was back in her bedroom, she kept one eye on the door as she felt sure Billy would come up and try to make advances to her. She put on a pair of silk Charnos panties and stood doing her hair and face where she could see the bedroom door reflected in her mirror. If he'd come in, she'd been prepared to give him a real blast for his impertinence. By the time she'd finished beautifying herself, he still hadn't appeared. She'd decided to wear the Episode suit he'd sent her, and she'd put it on with just her panties, gold, low-heeled slingbacks, and Chanel "Coco". And he still hadn't barged in.

Why not? she wondered. Had the get-up she'd worn that day put him off, didn't he fancy her anymore? She'd decided it really was a bit much, all that show and no action. When she'd gone down, there he'd been, lazily reading the paper and drinking a Scotch. He'd complimented her on her looks in the new suit, and they'd had a most enjoyable supper together in the kitchen. During the evening, the visit to Cornwall had been agreed and they'd got on extremely well. They'd got on so well, and Caroline had fancied him so much, that she'd asked him if he'd like to stay the night, in a guest room, of course.

But he'd declined, saying, 'No, I'm not going to stay until you love me enough to want me in your own bed.' Then he'd held her in his arms, with his hard body pressed against hers, kissed her long and passionately, and then he'd just gone. She'd been left, literally panting, and cursing herself for letting him go.

Enough daydreaming. Turning in the car to admire his profile, she said, 'What do you really think about the Foundation, and what do you think will happen in San Francisco?'

'I've got a feeling that you were right in your summing up on Tuesday, but as Alastair said, we mustn't take any risks. We'll carry on as if we expect to tangle with a major international gang. That way we'll be prepared whatever the outcome. One thing we mustn't forget is the disappearance of those two girls. One could easily be explained, but two make it more difficult.'

'You're right, it's those two girls. I'll be quite ready for my lunch, having had such an early start.'

'It's a bit of a trek but we'll do it in about three hours. We could have flown down to Exeter but then there's all the hassle of getting a car.'

'The plane's repaired now, is it?'

'Yes, I got it back on Monday. We'll be in Okehampton in a minute. Would you like to stop for a coffee?'

'No thanks, unless you're desperate for one, I'd rather get there.'

'There's only one thing I'm desperate for and I've got her with me.'

'Oh, Billy, sometimes I think you're rather sweet,' she said, putting her hand on his thigh and giving it a gentle squeeze.

'I can put up with a lot of that. Shall I pull off the road?'

'No,' she said, laughing. 'Let's get there as quickly as possible, and I might even give you a kiss when we arrive.'

'What, of your own accord?'

'Yes, quite spontaneous.'

'I think the world is becoming a bright, new place.'

They continued their banter until they arrived in Boscastle, when Caroline had to give him directions on how to reach her parents' cottage which was up the hill at Forrabury Common.

Snuggly set in a well-sheltered garden, the cottage

was built of the usual Cornish granite blocks, softened by white painted doors and window frames, and climbing plants up the walls. In the autumn sun it looked mellow and welcoming.

'Here we are,' said Caroline. As Billy stopped the Porsche, she leant across, and taking his face gently in her hands, kissed him on the lips. 'Thank you for driving me down, and for being so nice to me.'

Before he could say, or do anything, they heard voices as Caroline's parents came out to meet them.

They all got on very well and Billy, who to start with, called Caroline's father respectfully "sir", was soon referring to him as "George". When she got the chance, Caroline's mother whispered to her, 'My dear, he's so handsome, elegant and charming.'

After they'd has a cup of coffee, George Johnson said, 'You must see our new conservatory, even Caroline hasn't seen it yet, have you, dear?'

'That's really nice,' Billy said, looking round it. 'I can see that'll be a great boon.'

'We wouldn't have it yet if it wasn't for Caroline, would we George? We'd budgeted for next spring, and then Caroline suddenly gave us two thousand pounds towards it that made all the difference. I expect she's told you all about it, but evidently, she was involved in some project at an Arab embassy, and all the people she met there were so vile she didn't want to keep the fee she was paid. So, in order to take the "nasty taste" away, she gave us the money for our conservatory.'

Billy looked at Caroline and they started to laugh uproariously. When they'd regained control of themselves, Mary Johnson looked puzzled. 'Did I say something funny?'

Caroline was still giggling. 'That's where Billy and I met. He was one of the nasties, if not the chief nasty.'

'Oh dear, I'm sorry, Billy. I'd no idea.'

'Please don't worry, Mary. As you can see, we're quite over that little problem.'

The Johnsons had decided it would be better to go down to the local hotel for luncheon so that Mary hadn't got to spend time preparing and serving it. They had a very good lunch, during which Caroline told her parents what a great time she'd had with the Grants, and how kind they'd been to her. George was very pleased to hear of Alexander Grant again, and to receive his message. As their table was discreetly placed, and she could not be overheard, Caroline told her parents about the work she was about to do for Alastair Brown. They were not over-pleased and, in fact, asked her to reconsider, and to withdraw from the project.

'Why on earth do you want to do it?' her father asked. 'Or get mixed up with Alastair Brown, of all people? You're doing very well with your features, and don't need the work. It can't be anything of great national importance or they'd be using full-time professionals. I can't see why you're putting yourself into this position, unless it's to help Billy.'

'Nothing to do with me, George. I've already suggested she pulls out.'

'Thank you both very much, can I get a word in? I'm doing it because I thought it would be an interesting adventure, and give me some very good material for a feature. Although I am now of the opinion that it isn't going to be a dangerous project, because it's concerned purely with a con, I would withdraw if I could.'

'Well, there's nothing to stop you dear, is there?' asked her mother.

'Yes, there is. I've agreed to do it and I can't let Alastair down.'

'I shouldn't worry too much about that, Caroline. He'd be quite liable to let you down if it suited his book,' Billy commented.

'That may be so, but that's him, not me.'

'Well, that's it, Billy. If Caroline thinks she's committed you'll never change her mind. She's always been like that, hasn't she Mary? Her word's her bond.'

Caroline looked at Billy and found he was surveying her with a quizzical look. 'That's more the code of a man than a woman,' he said.

'There Mum, have you ever come across a more chauvinistic man in your life?'

'Yes dear, your father.' They all laughed, and the subject was changed.

After lunch they had a short stroll in the village, went down to look at the small harbour and then back to the cottage. Caroline and Billy were asked if they'd stay the night but declined. They did, however, agree to stay and have a very early supper as Billy said that, as long as they left Boscastle by eight-thirty, he could have Caroline home by midnight.

During the afternoon, George and Billy sat in the conservatory and discussed their various "cloak-and-dagger" experiences. George, who had always been so reticent, seemed to enjoy discussing it all with Billy, and Caroline decided that perhaps either her father was mellowing, or that he felt a fellow feeling for Billy.

The two women spent most of the afternoon chatting upstairs in Mary's bedroom and looking at clothes. During the afternoon, Caroline's mother commented, 'I do like Billy, and I can tell your father does too. He's one of the nicest young men I've met for a long time. What is the situation between you? Are you serious?'

'I don't know yet, Mum. It's too early to tell.'

'You're not living together?'

'No, nothing like that. Having been married once I'm really looking for something more long-term than an affair.'

'I don't think it would do you any harm, dear. After all, John was a very serious man and, in some ways, I would imagine, difficult, so some time, even if it was not permanent, with a man as worldly and amusing as Billy would probably do you a lot of good.'

Caroline was quite thrown by hearing this suggestion from a mother who she'd always thought of as rather staid and strait-laced. 'Do you really think so, Mum?'

'Your father and I, although we liked him, were always worried that John, being much older than you and stuck in his ways, would make you old before your time. With Billy it would be the opposite. I even think that if I spent some time with Billy, I'd feel young again.'

What next, thought Caroline as she hugged and kissed her mother. 'Oh, Mum, you are a laugh, I can see I'll have to keep an eye on you.'

'You'd better not tell your father what I said as, thank God, he's still rather keen on me, and also a little jealous at times.'

Caroline laughed again and concluded that—what with finding out that her father had been a war hero and now all this—there was a lot she'd never known or understood about her parents.

By the time they left at eight, Billy and her parents were already the greatest of friends. There were promises of him visiting them again as soon as he could, and from them that they would let him fly them up to stay at the Grants' castle. Caroline almost felt left out as Billy seemed to be getting more fuss made of him than she was.

As they drove away and finished waving, Billy said, 'What charming parents you have. I'll look forward to seeing them again soon.'

'They certainly liked you, in fact, my mother quite fell for you.'

'A very intelligent woman your mother. You'd do well to follow her example.'

Yes, thought Caroline, *too true. I'm going to have you in my bed tonight, Mr Billy Grant, and hang the consequences.*

They ran into some heavy traffic before joining the motorway at Exeter, but after that the journey went well and they were in Oxford before midnight.

Caroline was excited at the thought of getting Billy into her bed, so as he drove up to her house she turned and smiling at him said, 'Why don't you park the car and come in, Billy?'

She could see by the way he turned and looked at her that he'd got the message. He didn't reply until he'd parked the car. 'Only if you really, truly want me to.'

'Yes, at this moment, there's nothing I want more.'

He turned in his seat, and leaning towards her, he kissed her. It was not so much a passionate kiss as a sensual one. They nibbled each other's lips, and their tongues caressed each other's. Then his hand moved up and covered her breast.

'Let's go into the house,' she whispered huskily.

When they got out of the car, he held her in his arms for a minute, and the feel of his body against hers made her mind reel with desire.

Crossing the dark road, they went up the steps to her front door, and as soon as she opened it, she knew there was something wrong. A shadowy figure appeared in front of them in the hall and a gruff voice said in a quiet, sinister voice, 'Right you two, lie face down, and don't say anything and you won't be hurt.'

She didn't really see Billy move. There was just a sort of blur and then the shadowy figure gave a short yelp of pain and crashed to the floor. Caroline then knew what Alastair had meant when he'd said, 'Billy is the best when there's trouble.'

It had all happened in a flash, and then Billy was beside her, whispering in her ear, 'There's someone else upstairs. Go to one of your neighbours' and call the police. Tell them these men are armed.' Then of all things, he kissed her, after which he gently pushed her out of the front door. As she went, she heard someone from the upper part of the house call out in a subdued voice, 'Or-roight, Jim, are you or-roight?'

As the lights were on in the next house but one Caroline went straight there and rang the doorbell. Richard and Mary who lived there were friends and took her straight to the phone. Whilst she was dialling 999, they heard a gunshot coming from the direction of her house.

'Shotgun,' said Richard. 'What shall we do?'

Caroline quickly gave details of what was happening,

and where, to the operator who said police would be with them in a few minutes.

'I'm going to go back and see if I can help Billy,' she said.

'I'll come with you. You stay here, Mary.'

As they went gingerly towards Caroline's house, the door opened, and Billy appeared and waved them back. 'Go back into the other house and wait,' he called out to them.

Caroline didn't like leaving him, but she thought it better to follow his instructions. She and Richard had only just got back there when two police cars screamed into the road, with all their flashers going and pulled up outside Caroline's house.

Men tumbled out, some running back up the road, and down the access to the rear of the house, and others covering the house from all angles. Caroline saw Billy come out of her front door, he wasn't taking any chances, he had his hands up. He spoke for a couple of minutes to the police officer who was in charge and then they all stormed back into the house. After another few minutes an ambulance appeared and stopped a short way from Caroline's house. Then the lights in her house went on, and she thought it time for her to go and see how Billy was, and what was happening. As she got there, another police car arrived and a senior-looking man, in plain clothes, got out. Billy and a uniformed police officer came out to meet this new arrival.

Billy, seeing Caroline, went over to her and taking her by the hand, led her over to the police and introduced her as the owner of the house. They then all went into the drawing room and Billy was asked to explain what had happened. He told them how he'd been bringing Caroline home and how they'd been received when they entered the house. He then went on to explain what had happened after he sent her off to phone.

'When Mrs Dalglish had left,' he said, 'an accomplice called out from the top of the house, and then started to come downstairs. As he passed the landing window, I could make out that he was carrying a sawn-off shotgun, so I needed to deal with him without delay. It was easy, I just waited beside the dark staircase, and as he came down grabbed his leg through the banisters, he tripped, fired a shot, and fell to the bottom of the stairs. I thought there might be another man upstairs, that's why I didn't want anyone else in until you arrived.'

At that moment, a policeman came in from the kitchen. 'Can we send them off in the ambulance now, sir?'

'Yes, incidentally, what's wrong with them?'

'One's got a broken collarbone and suspected concussion and the other's got a broken leg and again, suspected concussion.'

'Now I recognise who you are, sir. Major Billy Grant, isn't it?' asked the man in plain clothes.

'Yes, but it's Mr now. We've met before?'

'Yes, sir. You gave a lecture at an anti-terrorist course I was on. Now, Mrs Dalglish, we'll need a statement from you, but the morning will do. We've got things to do here, and the place is a bit of a mess, is there somewhere nearby where you can stay tonight?'

Richard and Mary, who'd come in to see if they could help, said in unison, 'With us.'

Caroline look wistfully at Billy, he pulled a wry face and said, 'That's very kind, and the ideal thing for you, Caroline, as it's already gone two.' Then he turned to the policeman. 'I'll come and make my statement now, as I'm tied up all tomorrow.'

Oh, damn, damn, damn, thought Caroline, *I'm not going to have him tonight nor, obviously, see him tomorrow. Those blasted robbers have wrecked more than my home.*

Caroline went up to her room to collect a few things for the night and was horrified by the mess, although it was all superficial: drawers open, contents spewed on the floor etc.

When she got back downstairs and was about to leave, the senior policeman said to her, 'What a bit of luck you had Major Grant with you. We know these two, and they're very unpleasant, dangerous men. We've been after them for months, ever since Jim, the leader, left jail. They're wanted for robbery with violence, rape and possibly even murder.'

Caroline shuddered, if she'd just said goodnight to Billy in the car and gone into the house on her own, anything could have happened.

Richard and Mary having gone back to their house, Billy took the chance of walking there with her. On the doorstep, he took her gently in his arms and kissed her. Then looking deeply into her eyes, said, 'What a day it's been, darling. I feel I've learnt more about you in the last few hours than I had in the previous few weeks. I'm devastated when I think what I've missed because of those two pigs. I could kill them. I hope the whole thing hasn't upset you too much?'

'Billy, how do I thank you for what you did? You may well have saved my life, or at the very least from a very nasty time.'

'You don't have to thank me, darling, I'm beginning to think I'd do anything for you.'

The door opened and Richard looked out. 'Oh sorry, just wondered if you're ready, Caroline, so that we can all get to bed?' he said.

When Caroline was in bed, she lay back thinking about the day, and how wonderful Billy had been; not just in dealing with the villains but during the whole day. Her parents liking him so much, and her mother putting her seal of approval on him, had meant a lot to her. Although she was a woman in her own right, and made her own decisions, and was not answerable to anyone, their approval still meant a lot to her. Billy, she was now convinced, was not just lusting for her body, she giggled, he was lusting for all of her.

She didn't wake the next morning until Mary brought her a cup of tea, just before ten, when she jumped out of bed in a great rush. When she walked down to her house, the police had gone but her daily was there, clucking away as she tidied everything up and put stuff back where it belonged. Caroline went straight into her study to listen to her answerphone. There was a message from Alastair Brown asking her to call him without delay. Then there was one she'd hoped there might be, Billy's voice saying, 'Hello adorable, this is Billy at just before five AM. I've given my statement to the police and am just about to go home. I only wish I was coming back to snuggle up in your bed with you, but no luck, I'm on my way to London. I've got a very full day in front of me, but I'll ring you sometime. Hope you had a good night's sleep. Love you, darling.'

Caroline sat all hunched up with her fists clenched, did he really mean *I love you*, or was he just using it as a meaningless expression of affection? He'd never said it before, and he'd only ever called her darling three times before, and one of those didn't count anyway. She wished she could see him. She wished even more that she could hold him in her arms. When would he call her, when would she see him again?

The phone rang, it was Alastair.

'Alastair, sorry I didn't call you back yesterday, I was just about to now.'

'I've just heard about your trouble last night. Hope you're all right.'

'Yes, fine thanks. Billy called you, did he?'

'No, my dear, I heard from another source. What I wanted you for is that you've a letter from our friends. They want you to make your way to San Francisco early next week. Doesn't give much time, does it? Do you think you can make it?'

'That's going to mean leaving Saturday or Sunday, isn't it?'

'Yes. You want to have a bit of time to settle in before it all starts.'

'I just can't make it by tomorrow. It'll have to be Sunday. What about Billy?'

'I haven't been able to raise him yet, he's gone off somewhere, and for once we can't contact him, but his office will get him to call me as soon as they find him.'

'I'll plan to leave on Sunday, can you let me have all the flight details etc?'

'Yes, my dear, I'll come back to you later today.'

When he'd cleared, Caroline started to list what she'd have to do before she left on Sunday. The list frightened her. She'd never get it all done.

She seemed to spend the rest of the morning on the phone. Several calls from Alastair, concerning San Francisco. She called her parents to thank them for the previous day, and to tell them what had happened when she got home, and that she was going on Sunday. A call to her builder to arrange for her hall ceiling to be repaired after the shotgun blast. Then a policeman arrived to take her statement, and that was the end of the morning.

In the afternoon, a courier arrived from Alastair with air tickets, a hotel booking confirmation fax and a big wad of dollars and travellers' cheques.

There was also a photostat of the letter to her from the Foundation, which was brief and to the point. It thanked her for going to see Charles and gave her a number in San Francisco to telephone when she arrived there. There was no mention, or thanks, for the thousand pounds she'd donated!

The British Airways ticket was for first-class seat number 1A on BA 287 departing Heathrow at 13:15 with an ETA, San Francisco of 16:15, local time.

The hotel booking was for a deluxe single room at the Hyatt at Fisherman's Wharf, for a week. Alastair had explained that, although they only expected her to stay there a night or two, it was being kept as a bolt hole, in case she suddenly needed one.

She still hadn't heard from Billy, where on earth had he got to? She needed a blow of fresh air and a short walk, but she didn't dare leave the house in case he phoned. When at eight she was beginning to give up ever hearing from him again the phone rang, and it was him.

'Hello, darling, how are you?'

'Billy, I'd almost given you up.'

'Have you missed me?'

'Yes, very much.'

'Hearing you say that has made my day; I was feeling a bit tired and depressed, but now I feel great, and on top of the world again. I've just been longing to see you all day, and instead of concentrating on the job in hand, I've kept thinking about you.'

'Am I going to see you tonight?'

'No, darling, you're not. I'm in Geneva. I had to come over unexpectedly this morning. I'm frantically trying to finish my negotiations with these people before we go to San Francisco. I don't think I've got a chance of getting back until late tomorrow, or maybe even Sunday, just in time to catch our plane. It's made me mad. I want to be with you.'

'I desperately want to be with you too, but I quite understand, there will be plenty of time when we've got this job done, won't there?'

'That's one thing you can be sure of. Let's go to Scotland as soon as we get back, and go for a week's cruise on *Lake Windrush*, she's got central heating and everything, ending up back at the castle, in time for the ball.'

'Oh yes, Billy, that sounds so romantic it just makes

me squirm to think of it. How long before we're back, about a week?'

'I should think so, but however long will be too long. I want you now, Caroline, right now.'

'I know, I can't wait either.'

'I think we'd better change the subject before I blow my top. You've received your tickets and everything … fine. I'll be on the same plane in the next seat—B1. It would be better if we didn't appear to know one another and just to have met on the plane as fellow passengers. Stan will collect you in the "taxi" and take you to Heathrow, but at the other end you'll have to find a cab to take you to the hotel as it would be better if we arrived independently, but we'll be able to talk on the house phone as soon as we arrive. I feel sure all these precautions will be proved to be unnecessary, but we must treat this as a serious, dangerous operation, until we definitely know otherwise, or have to bust it.'

'Yes, I understand, and I respect you for it.'

'I think that covers everything for the moment and anyway I may get back in time to see you before we go, although I doubt it. Promise me one thing, that you'll take great care, and if anything seems to be going wrong, just think of yourself and get out.'

'Yes, I promise, Billy. There's one thing I must say to you, I'm fast falling deeply in love with you, if you're fooling with me, please stop now, and back off.'

'There's nothing fooling about the way I feel for you. I love you, darling, love you, love you. It's all been so quick, and now I'm so certain. I can't wait to be with you.'

When at last they'd managed to say goodbye to each other, Caroline was bursting with happiness. *He loves me,* she thought, *he actually loves me.*

CHAPTER TEN

Caroline was one of the earliest passengers to enter the first-class cabin of San Francisco-bound 747 and was already settled when the woman booked in the seat across the aisle arrived.

Caroline looked up at her, an attractive, dark, middle-aged woman, and said, 'Hello.'

'Hi, how do I get this God damn bag in the locker?'

'Let me help you, madam, if you'll just give me the bag and sit down.'

Nice looking, polite steward, thought Caroline, as the American lady collapsed into her seat, and the steward dealt with her bag.

A stewardess came up and asked Caroline what she'd

like as a pre-take-off drink. She chose champagne.

Caroline stood up, pretending to organise her things but, in reality, to look round the cabin to see what her fellow passengers looked like. Not very exciting, and none of them looked sinister.

Where was Billy? He should have arrived by now as it was getting near take-off time. She sat down as her drink arrived, and while sipping it, wondered what had happened to him and prayed he wouldn't miss the flight.

The American lady kept getting up and down and re-arranging her things and making amusing comments until she let out a low whistle.

'Look what's arrived. Now, honey, that's what I call a real dishy guy. Hope he's going to sit next to me.'

Caroline half stood up and looked back down the plane. Yes, just as she'd thought, it was Billy. He was, of course, surrounded by cabin crew who were talking and laughing with him and treating him as "someone special"—and he was. As Caroline watched him, she felt a wave of desire pulsate through her, he was so tall, handsome and full of vitality.

As he came up to the front of the compartment, with *two* stewardesses carrying his in-flight bag and magazines, the American lady preened herself hoping he was booked in the empty seat beside her and looked quite disgruntled when he said to Caroline, 'Hello, this must be me, I'm B1.'

Caroline looked up at him in as uninterested manner as she could achieve and said in a neutral voice, 'Hello.'

As soon as Billy was settled in his seat, they brought him a drink and, almost immediately, the announcement was made that they were about to take off.

Billy managed to give Caroline's arm a squeeze as he arranged his seatbelt but, other than that, they almost ignored each other until everyone was engaged eating lunch, when Billy at last felt it safe to concentrate on her.

'You look wonderful, I could hardly stop myself from taking you in my arms and kissing your delicious lips.'

'Oh, Billy, I wish you had.'

'I'm almost sure that there isn't anyone even remotely connected with the Foundation on this plane, but we just can't take the risk.'

'Does that mean that we can't be seen together in San Francisco, and will have to go our own separate ways?'

'No, I don't think so. We can dine together etc. If anyone sees us and asks you about it later you can say that we met on the plane, and that we bumped into each other again at the hotel, when I invited you to dine with me.'

'Of course, great. I am, according to my cover story, a

lonely widow desperately looking for friends, so I found one on the plane.'

They looked into each other's eyes and laughed.

The American lady leant across the isle and tapped Billy on the shoulder. 'You two seem to be getting on well,' she said in a slightly accusing voice.

'Yes, we've found lots of people and places that we both know.'

After lunch, Billy spent a bit of time sitting next to the American, talking to her, in order to create the impression that he was a friendly traveller who liked to meet his fellow passengers.

The flight passed very quickly, and Caroline was quite surprised when the announcement was made that they were approaching San Francisco.

After they had landed, she and Billy parted in a friendly manner, calling out to each other that they hoped they'd meet again.

She got herself a porter, who found her a cab, and then she was on her way into the city.

The sun was shining, and Caroline was excited to be in San Francisco again. It was some years since her last visit. John had sent her to check on some records for him when she was still his assistant. She'd loved it then, the way it was perched on hills above the Bay. She remembered the fun she'd had riding on the remaining cable cars, with the sudden panoramic views as you crested a hill, and the Bay itself with the Golden Gate Bridge. Within twenty minutes she was at the hotel and within a few minutes of that, in her room. The adventure had started in earnest. It was even more exciting than when she'd gone to Afghanistan, but that was purely because Billy was involved. Whatever she did with Billy would be exciting. She wondered where he was now. Had he arrived at the hotel yet? She didn't have to wait long to find out as at that moment her phone buzzed.

'Caroline, darling; everything okay?'

'No.'

'Why, what's wrong?' he asked urgently.

'You're not here with me, holding me in your arms.'

'Oh, darling, don't, I'm trying to unpack and get myself sorted out before I concentrate one hundred per cent on you.'

'Aren't you coming to my room?'

'Don't you want to unpack first?'

'No.'

'I'm on my way, open the door when I tap.'

Caroline put the receiver down with trembling hands

and wondered if she would be able to get to the door as her legs felts weak and her heart was thumping so much she was almost breathless.

There was a tap on the door, and she was there with a rush to open it and let Billy in.

He closed the door behind him and leant against it just looking at her and not moving. 'I just can't believe you are so beautiful. I keep thinking I must be dreaming. I've got to touch you to see if you are real.'

He stretched out his hands and placed them on her shoulders, which he caressed, and moving his hands down her arms, he gently drew her towards him until she could feel his masculine body, hard and strong, against hers. She could feel the fire in her own body, and she knew she was in the grip of lustful forces that she could no longer hold in check. She was out of control. She tilted her face towards his and their lips met. His tongue felt sensuous as it explored every part of her mouth, and then tremendously sexually arousing as he thrust it deeply in and out.

She shuddered, her breasts seemed to expand and her nipples to get even harder as she became hot, moist and unable to wait any longer.

They parted and moved into the room when, with

a strange-sounding cry, she literally tore off her clothes before throwing herself, spreadeagled, onto the bed.

She didn't care what he thought of her. She didn't care how she appeared. She didn't care what she had to do so long as he would satisfy the sexual craving of her body.

Through a mist she saw him standing by the bed struggling out of his clothes, then he stood before her, his tanned, muscular body naked and fully aroused.

She leant forward, stroked and caressed him, marvelled at his hardness and then cried out in a strangled voice, 'Please, darling ... please!'

She felt his lips and tongue caressing her nipples and breasts and then start to explore the rest of her body until she was gasping for breath and almost sobbing. At last, as her hot juices flowed, moving over her and between her outstretched legs, he entered her. Gently at first, barely penetrating her, but as the momentum gathered pace, going ever harder and deeper.

She couldn't believe it. She had never experienced anything like it before. Her whole body was tensed up as she met thrust for thrust. She wanted him ever deeper. She wanted to feel every inch of his body against hers. She was like a volcano on the edge of erupting. Then she did erupt, she cried out as her sense reeled and she felt as though her body was filled with molten lava. Billy gave a great sigh and rolled over beside her where they stayed for a few minutes as Billy kissed her and whispered sweet nothings to her.

Caroline lay there feeling fulfilled and content. It had been magic. She would never have believed that it could be such an experience, but then Billy was something special. So, it had to be.

As they kissed, Caroline felt a knot of fresh desire in her stomach. She pushed her tongue into Billy's mouth, but he moved back, laughing. 'Don't do that, darling, or you'll have me all rampages again.'

'That's what I'd hoped.'

'Don't tempt me. It's already nearly eight and we've got to unpack. I've got to phone in, and then I was going to take you out to dinner. Of course, when we get back after dinner, that'll be another matter.'

'Promises, promises.'

They laughed together and Billy ran his hand over Caroline's breast, across her stomach and down to her thighs.

'Wow! You'd better stop that if you really want to go and eat.'

'Why don't we skip dinner, and everything else, and

get a plane to Tahiti?'

'If only we could, but we can't let everyone down, we must finish what we came out to do.'

'You're amazing, you're so dependable, you're not like the majority of women.'

'There you go again, didn't I just tell my mother how chauvinistic you were?' she said, giggling.

With an obvious effort, Billy let go of her and stepped back from the bed. 'I must make that phone call or there will be a panic.'

'Who have you got to call?'

'I've arranged some backup for us with an old CIA contact of mine and I promised to ring in when we arrived.'

'Right, you go and do that, and I'll unpack, make myself presentable, and then you can take me out to dinner.'

'Perfect, what shall we say, half an hour?'

'No way,' she answered laughingly, 'after what I've just been through, make it at least an hour.'

'All right, an hour, but I can't bear to be parted for longer than that.'

As Caroline got up off the bed, Billy stepped forward and took her in his arms, their naked bodies merged. A great wave of lust swept through her, and she wanted to do things to him that she had never done to any man before. She gradually sank to her knees, kissing and caressing his body as she slid down it. Then she licked and kissed the very centre of his manhood, at last sucking it into her mouth. She heard him gasp and his body was trembling with tension and desire. Her own desire was welling up inside her until she could stand it no longer and had to have him inside her again. Letting go of him, she lay back on the floor with her legs raised and spread wide.

'Again, darling ... now ... please,' she pleaded.

Kneeling, he placed her legs over his shoulders and plunged straight into her. Leaning forward he was able to kiss her before they were forced apart by their gyrating bodies as they reached an almighty climax. Rolling over they lay side by side with their bodies still united.

'Darling, you're mind-blowing. I knew you were warm and romantic, but I never guessed you were so passionate and red hot.'

'Don't you like me like that? Are you shocked?'

'Shocked? Not like you like that? You are magnificent, you are unbelievable, you are so desirable that you make my hair stand on end.'

'I didn't get the impression that it was your hair that was affected.'

They laughed together and kissed, and at last their bodies were parted.

'And now, my darling, you must go and make your phone call and we'll meet in one hour.'

'Yes, I suppose I must. We'd better meet downstairs as though we'd bumped into each other. There is a bar on the right, as you come out of the lift. It's got a big fireplace with chairs grouped round it. I'll sit there and when you come in, I'll recognise you and ask you to have a drink, and then dinner.'

'That sounds fine. What time shall I come down?'

'Ring my room, 250, as soon as you're ready, then I'll go down and you can follow a few minutes later. Now, I'd better put my clothes on before we get diverted again.'

After Billy had gone, Caroline sat for a few minutes smiling to herself and feeling happier than she could ever remember feeling before. What, she wondered, would be their future together? Was he thinking of just a long-term relationship or would he want to marry her? He had said he was serious—but how serious? There was no doubt in her mind she loved him and wanted to be with him forever.

Amazingly, she was ready within the hour, dressed in her black velvet Ralph Lauren shift dress, and was able to ring Billy to say so.

When she walked into the bar, a lot of heads turned to look at her. Seeing the fireplace to her left she sauntered towards it and Billy rose to his feet and walked towards her with outstretched hand.

'Fancy seeing you again. When we talked on the plane, I'd no idea you were staying here.'

'What a pleasant surprise. How nice to see you again.'

'Are you meeting someone, or can I get you a drink?'

'No, I'm alone. A drink would be very nice.'

They sat side by side on a sofa and chatted and sipped their drinks. No one seemed to be taking any particular interest in them.

'There's a seafood restaurant just along the wharf from here where I thought we might eat. No one can be on to us. It would be just pure bad luck if anyone from the Foundation saw you with me. Anyway, you've got a good story to cover that eventuality. I must say, Caroline, I'll be very relieved and happy when all this is over.'

'Don't worry, I'm sure everything will be all right. The more I think about it, the more certain I am that it's just a confidence trick.'

'I'm sure you're right, but the sooner we know for certain, and you're out of here, the better.'

After they'd had another drink, they went along Fisherman's Wharf to Castagnola's Restaurant where they sat at a table looking onto the water and moored fishing boats. Billy called for a bottle of champagne and they ordered fish dishes.

The lights were dim and the atmosphere romantic. Caroline felt good—really good. She felt relaxed and the tenseness that she usually suffered from was gone. She felt soft and—what was the word—voluptuous. She giggled.

Smiling at her, Billy asked, 'What's amusing you?'

'I was just wondering if I could be called voluptuous.'

'I'd go along with that. You are also gorgeous, delectable, very, very sexy looking, at time tantalising, and amazingly hot stuff.'

'Do you really think I'm hot stuff? I'm sure that compared to most women I'm not.'

'My dear, darling Caroline, how can you say that? The way you kissed and sucked me and laid back in a most uninhibited way, showing your all and crying out for me, was about as hot as you can get.'

'Billy, you're making me blush. Was I really as naughty

as that? It's only because I love you that I did any of it. It's not because I'm hot stuff, as you call it.'

'Darling, I know. I'm sorry, I was only joking. You have nothing to blush about. You were making love as it should be made between two people who love each other.'

Billy's hand, under cover of the table, slid under her skirt and caressed her bare thigh between stocking top and silk briefs. She was glad she'd worn stockings instead of tights. It felt so good. They sat and looked into each other's eyes, and she felt the stirring of desire—she wanted him again!

She had to clear her throat before she could speak, and even then, it sounded a bit hoarse. 'Shall we go back to the hotel now, Billy? It's getting quite late.'

'Yes, I think we'd better,' he said, grinning at her.

When they got back to their hotel, Caroline, as arranged, collected her key and went straight up to her room. Billy spent a few minutes in the foyer, then collecting his key, went up in the lift, and going to Caroline's door, tapped on it.

When he was inside, he found her waiting for him dressed in her Charnos briefs, black suspender belt, black silk stockings and black high-heeled courts—and nothing else!

'Am I being awfully naughty?' she asked, as she stood there flushed with desire.

He couldn't answer as his lips were already otherwise engaged.

During Monday they went out over the Golden Bridge by cab to see the fantastic view of San Francisco from the far side. They went to Union Square for lunch in a smart restaurant and they spent the afternoon and evening making love. Over dinner, which they had served in Billy's room, they agreed that the next morning Caroline must get down to the job she had come for.

First thing Tuesday morning, Caroline phoned the number she'd been given for the Foundation. The woman that answered seemed to know all about her and gave her an address to report to: The Sanctuary, Sacramento Street.

'I know that street,' Billy said. 'It's up on Nob Hill. Must be one of those big, old houses.'

They phoned down for a cab and for someone to come up for her case.

Before Billy left her room, he took her in his arms, and they hung onto each other as though they were never going to be together again.

'Be very careful, darling, and if it seems to be going wrong, just get out. Once you're outside the front door I, or someone else, will be there, twenty-four hours a day, to help you. Don't forget I love you and am not going to let anything happen to you.'

The house, as Billy had suspected, was large and oldish. The door was opened by a very pleasant woman, who appeared to Caroline, to be in her late thirties. 'You're Caroline … yes, I'm Martha. The Master has asked me to show you to your cell, and then to show you round before taking you for an audience with him.'

Her "cell" turned out to be a plain, but comfortably furnished, single room. Leaving her suitcase, she was taken by Martha to see the rest of the house. The interior was all painted white, the floors were parquet, and the furniture was mainly pine. In one very large room there was a group of people playing guitars and singing a folksy song. Some of them waved as the two women put their heads round the door. There was another large room that was set out as a chapel, and in there were several people, both men and women, who were on their knees, presumably praying. There were other rooms—sitting rooms, a dining room, another music room, kitchens— and one solid locked door which Caroline was told was the punishment room. She saw quite a few people as she went round and they all smiled and seemed friendly, and in good spirits. She and Martha ended up outside an impressive mahogany door where Martha paused, and as she knocked on it hesitatingly, said to Caroline in a hushed voice, 'This is the Master's sanctum.'

A voice from within called out, 'Enter.'

Inside, in a luxurious office, was a fat, jovial man who smiled at her and offered her a seat. Over the next two hours or so he told Caroline the aims of the Foundation and what one had to do. Caroline knew by the end of this time that she'd been right, this was just a set-up to take money off people. He went on about their expansion and how they were looking for one or two likely people to start a "Sanctuary" in the UK: a nice old historic house somewhere in the Buckinghamshire/Hertfordshire area. Charles had evidently reported that he thought she would be a good candidate to help set up the new "Sanctuary". Caroline carried on the conversation as though she was interested, but thinking to herself that she was off the hook and could leave whenever she was ready, as she had done her job. Then she remembered the two girls who had disappeared, and she decided that she must try to find out something about them before she left. Outside the Master's door, Martha was waiting to take her to the refectory for some lunch.

Over lunch, she found out that Martha had been there for some time. Caroline managed to bring into the conversation that a girl she knew, Joan Taylor, who was one of the two who had disappeared, had come to the "Sanctuary" and she wondered what had happened to her. Martha gave her a startled look and said, 'We wonder that as well.'

'You mean she just disappeared?'

'Yes, that's more or less what happened. She *was* just about to go back to England and needed some of our literature to take with her. We don't keep the bulk of that stuff here. It's still in a room we kept for ourselves, in the old warehouse where we started. Other people now rent the building, although it's still in our name. We're meant to go on Fridays, at ten, if we want to collect something, when there's someone there to see us in and out. Joan had suddenly decided to leave on a Tuesday and wanted some literature so, as we still had some old keys, she went down under her own steam. We've never seen her since. We asked the people at the warehouse if they'd seen her, and reported it to the police, but none of them took much notice. I think the police list us as a strange bunch that anything could happen to.'

'What a very odd thing to happen.'

'Yes, but even stranger was that the same thing

happened, in exactly the same circumstances, to another girl, named Alice.'

'Didn't the police think it strange that it happened a second time?'

'I don't know whether the Master even reported the second one as he'd been rather laughed at, at the time of Joan.'

Caroline didn't like the sound of that too much but said no more and changed the subject.

Caroline spent that night in her little "cell" thinking about Billy and what they'd done together, and wishing he was there, in bed with her.

The next morning, Caroline saw the Master and told him she was very interested in his proposal for the UK, but would have to go home and think about it for a while. He agreed.

Caroline found Martha and told her, 'I'm going home. You've heard I may be starting a "Sanctuary" in England? I'll need to collect some of your literature to take back with me. Can you let me have a key to the warehouse?'

Martha wasn't too keen but eventually she agreed, and, getting one for Caroline, gave her the address which turned out to be, at the back of the old piers, down by Fisherman's Wharf.

When Caroline walked out of the front door of the Sanctuary into Sacramento Street, she took a long, deep breath. She seemed to have been incarcerated for weeks. She started to walk down the street waiting to see what happened. Would Billy appear or was he in some hotel having a quiet drink? *No, that's not fair,* she thought, *he'll be around.*

A cab drew alongside, and the driver called out, 'Hi there, Caroline, Billy's waiting for you down the street, get on in.'

He turned left by Grace Cathedral and stopped. The door opened and Billy got in.

'Hello, darling, God, I've missed you,' he said, and kissed her. 'Everything all right?'

'Yes, apart from hating not being with you. I'm now one hundred per cent certain that it's just what we thought, a con set-up and nothing more. I've found out a bit about the two girls who went missing, and I think it may have something to do with the warehouse the Foundation use to store their literature. Both girls went there on their own, to collect literature, and were never seen again. Maybe there's some man living, or working, near the place who has carried them off. That's only pure guesswork, but I can't think of anything else. Anyway,

I've got a key, so we could go and have a look, if you think it's worth it.'

'Yes, why not? That will just tidy everything up and we can go home.'

The "taxi" dropped them at the door of the warehouse, and Billy thanked the driver for his help. 'You might as well report back now, we'll be okay. We'll get a real taxi when we've had a quick look inside.'

CHAPTER ELEVEN

Caroline unlocked the wicket gate and they went into the large, dank building. She didn't like it. It seemed spooky to her. Martha had told her where the Foundation's room was situated, so she went off to find it, while Billy nosed around generally. As she was in the Foundation's room looking at their literature, she could hear Billy banging away at something in the distance. Then she thought she heard the wicket gate slam but decided it couldn't be as Billy wouldn't go outside without her. When she came out of the room, the place was in silence, and she wasn't sure where Billy was, so she shouted.

'Billy, where are you?'

There was no reply—just silence.

She called again—still nothing.

She walked through the warehouse in the direction which she thought the banging had come from. She came to a door leading into another part of the building and saw an open packing case. Was this what Billy had been banging open?

She looked inside the box, and to her surprise it was full of guns, machine guns, the type they had had in Afghanistan.

There were lots of similar packing cases all round. She didn't like it; she didn't like it one little bit.

She called out for Billy again, and again. Nothing but silence. Then a figure appeared from among the packing cases, a large, unshaven, black-haired, rough-looking man.

'This way, miss,' he said in a gruff voice, a voice with some sort of accent. He beckoned her as he moved off across the warehouse.

Who was he, another of Billy's helpers? There was nothing for it. She'd have to follow him and hope he was leading her to Billy.

They went through a door and into another building filled with similar packing cases. She was just going to call out to the man hurrying along in front of her, when they came to the end of the packing cases and there was Billy.

He was a crumpled heap on the floor with blood running down his face.

She turned to make a dash for the door but a man, who was holding a pistol, had moved up behind her.

'Okay, baby, nothing foolish.'

'What have you done to him?' she demanded in the most authoritative voice she could muster.

'Nothing yet, baby.'

Why did he keep calling her "baby" in that menacing voice? She moved towards Billy's slumped body. The man who had spoken stepped forward, and struck her violently across the face, saying, 'You move when you're told, and not before.'

She staggered and put her hand to her smarting face, opened her mouth to say something, and then thought better of it.

'Okay, Sam, tie 'em up. Use the chain on that guy's legs.'

Caroline stood helpless and watched as they put a chain first round one of Billy's ankles and then the other and locked it with a padlock. It must have caused him a lot of pain, as even though he was unconscious, he groaned. Then they tied his wrists behind his back with a length of rope and, rolling his handkerchief, inserted it between his lips and tied it behind his head. Billy groaned and opened his eyes, the man called Sam kicked him several times in the ribs, and Billy passed out again.

Caroline tried to get to him, but they stopped her.

'What I want to know now,' said the man who was obviously in charge, 'is who you are and where you come from?'

'Until you untie my friend, I don't intend to tell you anything.'

'Like hell. I want to know everything about you two, and what you're doing in my warehouse.'

'It's not your warehouse.'

'I ain't going to stand here and discuss who owns this building. Just tell me what I want to know. Sam, tie her hands behind her back.'

Caroline struggled as two men got hold of her, but it was no use, they soon had her hands tightly tied.

'Now, are you going to tell me what I want to know?'

'No.'

He stepped forward and before she realised what was happening, he had wound a piece of rope round her neck which he started to pull tight. Caroline gasped and choked—she couldn't breathe. Her lungs seemed about to burst, her head swam, and she could feel tears running down her cheeks. The rope was loosened.

'Okay, baby, want some more? Or are you going to tell daddy-o what he wants to know? After all, it ain't much. It's just who you are and why you two are in my warehouse.'

Caroline decided it was time to talk, but for the moment she couldn't. She leant forward and took large, gasping breaths. She would have liked to wipe the tears from her face but, with her hands tied behind her back, she couldn't.

'All right,' she croaked, still gasping for breath. 'Give me a minute and I'll tell you.'

'Baby, I want to know and right now.'

She cleared her throat, she found it difficult to speak partially because of what he'd done to her, but mainly because she was so terrified. What was going to happen to Billy and her?

'We've come down from the Foundation to collect some literature.'

'Okay, so you've come from the Foundation. So, why on the wrong day and what the hell are you doing in my part of the building?'

'I'm sorry.'

'It ain't no use your being sorry. If that's all there is to it, why didn't you say that straight away instead of refusing to talk?'

'Because when I saw my friend on the floor, I thought you must be burglars who had broken in.'

'What are you, a limey?'

'Yes, if by that you mean English?'

'I don't go for what you're saying. That guy ain't no screwy nut from the Foundation. He's too tough and smart. We had a job to deal with him.'

What should she say? Caroline didn't know but then she thought the best thing was just to follow their cover story.

'No, you're quite right, he's not anything to do with the Foundation, I met him on the plane coming out from England and we've been seeing each other since I've been here.'

'So, what does the guy do?'

'I don't know, just a businessman of some sort.'

'Lady, I don't believe you, but there's no time now. We'll find out all about the two of you later.'

Then they gagged her, pushed her to the floor and tied her ankles with more rope. The man who seemed to be the leader, said, 'Don't worry, doll, if you don't think you're getting enough attention we'll put that right later, won't we boys?' They all laughed in a coarse, frightening way.

'Sam, you and Jake take them out to the caravan on the plantation where we can question them later. Get back here pronto as we have a consignment to ship out today. We must also be prepared to move everything elsewhere if it appears that these two guys could cause a threat to us. See if it's all clear at the side entrance and we'll get them into the car. Put the guy in the trunk and the dame on the floor in the back.'

As they dragged them out, Caroline saw they took the opportunity to give Billy a few more kicks. The leader said, 'You'll be sorry you stumbled on this lot, our IRA and Red Brigade friends wouldn't like that at all. The last two women we found here gave us some fun, didn't they boys? Though one of them didn't last long. Not much stamina.' They all laughed grotesquely.

Caroline didn't know how long they'd been driving, she'd lost count of time, when the car eventually stopped. They pulled her out of the back simply by grabbing hold of her hair and pulling. They lifted her up and shoved her roughly through the door of a small caravan, and then they appeared with Billy. When she and Billy were lying on the floor, side by side, the one called Jake said, 'What about a quick one with her now, Sam?'

'No, plenty of time for that this evening. We'd better get back.'

Sam gave Billy a couple more kicks as they shut the door and left.

Caroline could hear the car as it drove away, and then silence. After a few minutes Billy rolled over and turned towards her. *My God,* she thought, *what a mess.* His face was covered with blood, one eye was already closed and what she could see of his face was turning black and blue. With his one good eye he managed to give her a wink, and then by rolling his body he made her see he wanted her to roll over; then he followed suit, and she felt his fingers trying to undo the rope round her wrists.

She didn't know how long they lay like that, with Billy working away all the time, but it must have been at the very least an hour, when she suddenly felt the rope slacken. She pulled hard for a few minutes and then her wrists were free. She couldn't believe it, she massaged her wrists until some life came back into them, and then she rolled over and undid Billy's. When they both removed their gags, they turned and looked at each other, she wanted to kiss him, but she didn't know where, his face was such a mess. He put his arm round her, as they sat on the floor, and just held her for a minute.

'Untie your ankles, Caroline.'

While she was doing that, he rolled over to the door, which was locked, and bringing his feet up, kicked it off its hinges. Caroline saw that this effort had exhausted him, and she realised he must be badly injured.

He turned to look at her again. 'I want you out of here. It will be dark soon, so make your way down the track and watch out for them coming back. If their car comes, just get into the bushes at the side of the road, and wait until they've gone past, then continue until you find someone to help you.'

'Where are you going to be while all this happens?'

'I'll be here. I can't come with you. My legs are chained so there's no way I could get them free or make it out of here.'

'If you're here when they get back, they'll kill you.'

'I can't help that. I'm only interested in getting you out safely.'

'Think again, Billy, I'm not leaving you.'

'Please Caroline, it's touch and go whether you live or die. This may be your only chance to escape.'

'No, touch and go or not, I'm staying with you.'

He lay there looking at her and she could tell he was

assessing her resolve.

'Right, if you won't go then we must get as far into those bushes as we can. This is obviously an old vineyard fallen into neglect. Those old vines will make a good hiding place.'

Caroline found a long-handled broom in a corner, which Billy used on one side as a crutch, and on the other Caroline. His legs were so tightly chained that he had to swing them together, something that normally he could have done easily but not now as he was badly injured and in great pain.

They scrabbled their way, Billy making them go down lines so that they didn't leave signs of where they'd gone. It was getting dark, and they'd only managed to get about a hundred and fifty yards from the caravan when the darkness was slashed by the lights of an approaching car. Three of the men were back. There was a great shout of rage and obscenities when they found that Caroline and Billy were gone. They could hear them discussing it and then one of them said, 'He's not got his leg chains off. They can't be far.'

One man moved the car so that the headlights shone out into the bushes, and then they walked out along the beam, searching as they went. On one or two occasions, when they thought they'd seen someone, there would be the roar of a shotgun. They gradually moved the car and Caroline could see that the strip of light was getting nearer and nearer to their hiding place. Very soon now it was going to illuminate where they were.

Then one of the men shouted, 'I've had enough of f— about like this, let's go and have a drink and wait for dawn. We'll find 'em easy enough then.'

The other two readily agreed, and one of them added, 'We could play poker for who has first go at the girl.' They laughed brutishly.

Caroline and Billy just lay in the bushes holding hands for a while as the noise from the caravan increased as large quantities of bourbon were drunk.

Then Billy whispered to Caroline, 'I want to ask you two things, darling.'

'Fire away, my dearest.'

'Now that they're very drunk and noisy, do you think you could get over to the car, and just see if they've left the ignition keys in it?'

'Surely they'd never do that?'

'Yes, from my experience, it's just the sort of thing they might do.'

'I can do that, no problem,' whispered Caroline,

trying to sound calm, as a sharp spear of fear stabbed her stomach. 'What's the other question?'

'Will you marry me?'

'Oh darling, of course I will. I didn't think you'd ever ask.'

'That makes me so happy. I was going to ask you before, but I wanted to wait for the right romantic moment, and what's more romantic than this? Under the stars, among the vines of California.'

'Oh Billy,' she said with tears in her eyes, and she just touched his poor broken lips with hers in the gentlest of kisses.

Then without more ado she was crawling towards the car. Her heart was in her mouth as she passed the caravan and thought what would happen if one of the three drunken villains should pick that minute to come outside. Those few hundred yards seemed to take forever and to be the most perilous journey of her life—which it probably was. Then she reached the car and joy upon joy Billy was right, the keys were in the ignition. She decided it would be better to leave the keys where they were in case one of the men came out to the car. Just as she was about to move away from the car, she noticed that there was something on the back seat. She looked again—she couldn't believe their luck. There, waiting to be taken by her, was a sawn-off shotgun and two boxes of shells. Somebody, she decided, was looking after them. She gingerly opened the door, not making a sound, picked up the gun and shells, and started back. But this time, because she was carrying the gun and cartridges, she was unable to crawl, so she went on a longer route to avoid passing too close to the caravan.

Back at base, Billy was lying where she'd left him, almost unconscious with pain, but he roused himself when she put her hand on his shoulder.

'I've got an engagement present for you, Billy,' she said, putting the shotgun and shells down in front of him.

'Great,' he whispered. 'That helps to even things up a bit. What about the car?'

'The key's in it.'

'Can you drive it? Is it automatic?'

'Yes, it is, and yes, I can.'

'This is the plan. I'll get nearer the caravan so that I can hold them for a while with the shotgun, while you drive off in the car.'

'If you think I'm leaving you here, darling, then you're out of your tiny little mind.'

'My dearest, darling Caroline, you must leave me. I just

can't make it to the car, and anyway the only important thing to me is to get you out of here.'

'So, the big, super macho hero can't get himself a few yards to the car because his legs are chained, and he's in a bit of discomfort. I can't go on my own. I'd never have the face to tell your father and all your friends how you threw in the sponge when the going got a bit tough.'

'Please go, darling.'

'No, I stay here, unless you come with me.'

There was a pregnant pause in their whispered conversation, and then Billy said, 'Right, how shall we do it?'

'The same way we got here, on your broomstick and me.'

'Okay, but I'll try and pull myself along the ground until we're clear of the bushes. Just one thing, promise me you'll leave me, and get away in the car if they catch on. Now I've got this gun I can give them a good run for their money.'

'Right,' she said, thinking, *Like hell!*

The noise from the caravan had ceased, and from the occasional grunt and snort, it appeared all three had fallen into a drunken sleep. Not quite so good for Caroline and Billy, as the previous noise would have drowned any they made.

After what seemed to Caroline like a lifetime, they reached the car and she helped Billy into the passenger seat, leaving the door open. Then she was in the driving seat and, crossing her fingers, turned the key. The engine fired immediately, she put the gear selector into D, they slammed their doors, and were off down the single-track farm road. She expected gunshots to follow them, but nothing happened. The noise they'd made couldn't have been enough to wake the drunken villains. She spoke to Billy but as he didn't answer she looked at him, he was unconscious after the strain of getting to the car. Caroline stopped the car just long enough to do up Billy's seatbelt so that he wouldn't slip off the seat, and to put the shotgun on the floor.

She felt exhilarated, even though she was desperately worried about Billy, they'd got away. She'd been much more scared than she'd ever been in Afghanistan, even though the risks there had been just as great. But then she hadn't minded too much if she lived or died, but now it was different—she'd got Billy.

The road was undulating and as she drove over one of the gentle slopes, she saw headlights coming along the track towards them.

'Oh no, no,' she shouted aloud. 'I can't bear it.' She stopped the car and sat there sobbing. 'There are more of them coming Billy,' she shouted to him, but he remained motionless. What, oh what, was she going to do? She couldn't go back; there was nowhere to go. As the car approached at high speed, she decided that the best thing she could do was to at least get it over quickly. If she got out, when the other car reached them and stopped, and stood in front of her car holding the shotgun in an aggressive manner, they would open fire and kill both her and Billy. At least they would die together, and hopefully quickly. Leaning across, she kissed the unconscious Billy on his lips and as the other car slid to a halt, got out and walked towards it, holding the shotgun aimed at it. Two figures emerged from the other car, and silhouetted by the headlights, one of them looked enormous, and both had guns. Then the big one shouted, 'For God's sake, put that gun down, Mrs D.'

'Fred, thank heavens.' And moving forward, they hugged each other.

'Where's the boss?'

'In the car, and badly hurt.'

She quickly gave Fred, and the man with him, the information they wanted, and she heard it being passed on over the radio. She also heard them ask for a chopper, with medical facilities and heavy-duty wire cutters, to come to their own location.

They made Billy as comfortable as they could, and as they waited, Fred told her how they'd lost them because Billy had let their undercover cab driver go, assuming it was all over.

'He shouldn't have done that,' Fred said. 'It was unlike him. He must have had his mind on other things. I'll give him a right old ticking-off for that.'

Luckily Fred, and the CIA agent, picked up the villain's car when it went back to the warehouse and had been able to work out where they must be being held.

As they were talking, a large helicopter passed overhead, and Fred said, 'That must be the CIA boys going to deal with your friends. What you uncovered, Mrs D, was a gun-running organisation that's been supplying terrorists for years. They were renting that warehouse as it was listed as being part of the Foundation and was, therefore, a very good cover. Just about every security force has been looking for them and look who found them, my very favourite lady.'

'That's nice of you, Fred, but I don't think I can really take all the credit. I didn't know you were over here, have you just arrived?'

'I came over the day before you in case the boss needed some backup. I've never known him so worried about an operation. I think he must consider you rather special, Mrs D.'

At last, the air ambulance arrived. They cut Billy's chains off, gave him some immediate first aid, and then flew him to San Francisco and hospital.

Billy was cleaned up and then taken straight into one of the operating theatres, so it was several hours before Caroline saw him again. When she was eventually allowed into his room, she couldn't see his face as it was swathed in bandages, and he was surrounded by tubes and wires and, being heavily sedated, was asleep.

She sat for a while just holding his hand until they suggested that it would be better if she went so that they could get on with certain things.

When Caroline left the hospital, she did so with a feeling of dread that Billy might never be the same again.

CHAPTER TWELVE

Caroline felt a little uneasy to be in Billy's Cessna again, especially as Billy wasn't there. She sat thinking about the last time she'd been in the plane, when it had been struck by lightning. What a flight that had been. Elizabeth was quite right when she said that wherever Billy was things seemed to happen.

The pilot, a nice young man called Nigel, who worked for Billy, broke into her thoughts, saying, 'Not long now. We should be at the castle in about half an hour or so.'

The castle! What was going to happen then?

She had seen Billy only once since he'd been flown out of San Francisco. He'd gone first to one of London's top hospitals, and then on to a Swiss sanatorium, where she'd eventually caught up with him.

Caroline had had to stay in the States for just over a week to give evidence at a court hearing. It had been a great frustration not being able to go back to England with Billy, but it was just one of those things that had to be done.

The CIA, who were responsible for looking after her, were very good and arranged to take her to see all the local sights, and places of interest. But there was only one sight she really wanted to see—Billy, fit and well.

She was, they told her, a top security risk as someone might try to have her "wasted", as they poetically put it, before she was able to give her evidence. This didn't exactly help her peace of mind which was already pretty shattered by worrying about Billy. However, as there had been nothing she could do about it she had sat back and made the most of it. She'd wondered what on earth John would have thought if he could have seen her being driven around downtown San Francisco in a large black limo with two, obviously heavily armed, bodyguards. Not his scene at all, he would have hated the very idea, but she'd bet herself that Billy would have a good laugh when she was able to describe it to him. She also thought he would enjoy hearing how Alastair Brown had flown over to, as he described it, debrief her. Most of the debriefing had taken place in exclusive restaurants over large and sumptuous meals, washed down with fine wine. His visit had cheered her up when he'd suddenly leant forward and said in a slightly slurred, conspiratorial voice, 'Caroline, I must say, well done, jolly good show, thanks from all concerned.' It had been good to see someone she knew and to hear his optimistic opinion that, to a man like Billy, the injuries he had received were insignificant.

After Alastair had gone back to the UK, Caroline had managed to do some shopping for presents to take home, including a beautiful silk and cashmere turtleneck sweater, from swanky Bullock & Jones of Union Square, for Billy.

Caroline and Elizabeth had kept in constant touch by phone, so she'd known that Billy's injuries consisted of fractured ribs, concussion, a serious eye injury and septicaemia. He'd had a brain scan which had shown that there was no long-term damage; his fractured ribs had not pierced his lungs; and his eye, which gave considerable worry as at first they'd thought he might lose the sight in it, had responded well to treatment. The septicaemia was caused by the wound from the rusty chain which had cut him to the bone. The doctors told Billy's father that it was only because Billy was so tough and fit, both physically and mentally, that he would recover fully without being left with any permanent disability.

When Caroline had finally got back to England, Billy had had his various operations and had been moved to a Swiss sanatorium for further treatment, and convalescence. She flew straight out there to see him. It was a very disappointing, unhappy visit. He was hardly ever available, as he was undergoing constant treatment of one sort or another, and even when she did see him, they were never alone. They didn't have a single chance to talk on a personal level.

In the meantime, neither Billy, nor anyone else, had mentioned their engagement and Caroline was beginning to wonder if he'd been too delirious, at the time, to remember that he'd asked her to marry him.

Elizabeth had been in touch about the ball and explained that Billy was not arriving back at the castle until the day before the party. Although Elizabeth had said that she would be welcome to arrive any time she liked, Caroline got the feeling that she was not wanted until the day of the ball. She'd wondered why, but surely it couldn't be anything ominous.

Billy had appeared a bit odd when she'd seen him in

Switzerland, but she thought at the time that that was because of the circumstances and nothing to do with their personal relationship. As the plane was, in any case, going to be tied up collecting Billy for a few days before the party, Caroline opted to fly up the afternoon of the ball.

She couldn't wait to see Billy, as her love had deepened over the weeks, but she was also rather frightened in case his injuries had changed him, and even more, in case he either didn't remember, or hadn't meant to ask her to marry him. If that was the case, she didn't know what she'd do. She just wouldn't be able to bear it. Her life, which had begun to look so good, would be shattered.

Looking out of her window, she saw they were passing over the Loch and knew it would only be a few minutes before they landed. As the plane flew in over the castle, she could see lots of vans in the courtyard, and flags flying from the flagpoles. They were getting ready for the ball.

When the plane touched down, she could see a Range Rover standing by the hangar but couldn't see who was with it. After the plane came to a halt and the engines had been turned off, the Range Rover drove across and stopped. She still couldn't see who was driving it. Nigel opened the door for her. 'Bye for now, see you later.'

Caroline stepped out onto the runway—and there was Billy—waiting for her. For a minute or two he just held her in his arms without saying or doing anything. Then he whispered in a low, husky voice, 'Darling, how I've missed you. Don't let's ever be parted again.'

As their lips met, Caroline knew he still loved her, and that she loved him more than ever. After a minute of close embrace, she stepped back to look at him, apart from some marks on his face, he looked just the same, her sweet, handsome, charming Billy.

'Oh, Billy, I've missed you so much. It's wonderful to be with you again.'

They clung to each other again until Billy said, 'Let me take you back to the castle. You'll need a cup of tea and some rest before you get ready for the ball.'

When they drove into the castle courtyard, Elizabeth and Alexander Grant, who must have been watching for them, came out to hug, kiss and welcome Caroline. As the castle was a hive of activity, they suggested a cup of tea in the turret sitting room after which Caroline would have a chance to rest and get ready at her leisure. They told her there was to be a small private party before the ball. As they were going into the castle, a voice from the background said, 'I'll tack the lassie's bag to yon pink room.' It was MacDonald, who actually smiled when Caroline acknowledged him.

When Caroline finally got to her bedroom, she found she'd only got about an hour and a half before the pre-ball party, just long enough to make herself as beautiful as possible. When she was in her bath, she just had time to think how fantastic it was to see Billy again, and to be back here with the Grants. But still no one had mentioned the engagement. She now felt sure Billy must have been too delirious to remember asking her. She decided there was nothing she could do, so she might just as well enjoy the evening and see what happened.

She'd had her hair titivated that morning, before she left Oxford, so it only needed tidying up, then she made-up carefully.

A frilly white suspender belt, black silk stockings, white silk briefs, black high-heeled courts, Chanel's "Coco" and she was ready for the dress she'd bought, regardless of expense, for this reunion with Billy. It was white, completely off the shoulders with a fitted, scalloped-topped bodice, tight waist and full ankle-length skirt. Round the waist was a broad, black silk sash with a centrally placed bow, which contained a white silk rose. Large pearl cluster earrings and black elbow-length gloves completed her ensemble. She looked in the mirror and was pleased by her reflection. Yes, very pleased.

She didn't know why, but she'd been asked to go down to the hall, where they were having drinks, at exactly twenty to eight. At twenty-one minutes to eight she thought she'd better make her way down.

As she approached the top of the stairs, she was surprised that there didn't seem to be any talking and laughing coming from the hall, but as she stepped out onto the stairs MacDonald's pipes started to play *Scotland the Brave*, and she saw in the hall below, a crowd of smartly dressed people, who all started to clap. She didn't know what to do, she couldn't understand it, and then she saw at the front of the crowd, beside the Grants, her parents, Alastair Brown and, bursting out of a dinner jacket, Fred.

When she was a few steps from the bottom, Lord Grant came up to meet her, and taking her hand, stopped her where she was.

Holding up his other hand for silence, he said, 'My friends, you've all heard about this young lady, and those of you who haven't met her before can see for yourselves that we've not exaggerated. She is unbelievably beautiful. What you can't see is that below all that beauty lies the most dependable and honourable person you could ever hope to meet. You've all heard of how she stood by Billy and refused to leave him to save her own skin when they were in a very dangerous and precarious situation. There is no doubt she saved Billy's life, and for that both Elizabeth and I will be eternally grateful. I'm going to ask you all to join me in raising your glasses in a toast to this most courageous of courageous young women, Caroline.'

Billy had come up beside his father to hand him a glass of champagne and they all raised their glasses and shouted, 'Caroline.'

Then Alexander Grant kissed her and so did Billy. While everyone was still clapping, Billy whispered to her, 'You haven't changed your mind, darling, you still want to marry me?'

Caroline could hardly find her voice she was so choked with emotion, but she managed to say, 'Yes, more than anything in the world.'

Billy, turning to Lord Grant and grinning like a Cheshire cat, said, 'It's all right, Father, she'll still have me.'

Lord Grant, now grinning just as broadly as Billy, again held up his hand for silence. 'It gives me, and both the families concerned, the greatest satisfaction and pleasure that I can now announce that Billy and Caroline are to be married. So, let's have another toast, to Caroline and Billy.'

Then Billy kissed her, and her parents hugged and kissed her, and so did everyone else.

She found out that her parents, and the other "special guests", had kept out of the way when she first arrived to add to her surprise when she came down to the party. That's why Elizabeth hadn't wanted Caroline to arrive before the actual day. Her parents had already been at the castle for three days and told her what a wonderful time they'd had with the Grants.

Alastair Brown, who actually kissed her on the cheek, told her that he'd submitted her name, "for a little something in the New Year's Honours' List", although he didn't know if anything would come of it.

'But that shouldn't be me, Alastair, it should be Billy.'

'No, my dear, you are the one who broke the terrorist arms supply. Anyway, if it hadn't been for you, both of you would have ended up, like those poor girls, in hillside graves.'

Then Fred came up and gave her a great big bear hug. 'I'll have to get used to calling you Mrs G now, won't I Mrs D? I'm real 'appy for you both. What a pair you'll make.'

And so it went on. What an evening it was. The dinner,

preceding the ball, was a never-to-be-forgotten occasion.

At the ball, all the men, including Andrew, wanted to dance with Caroline, and to tell her how proud they were of her, and how happy they were that she and Billy were to be wed.

Billy danced a bit, but his legs were still not quite back to normal. 'Otherwise,' he said to Caroline, 'I wouldn't let anyone else dance with you. So, you'd better make the most of it.'

Caroline had begun to feel like a "fairy princess", but by about one, she wanted to get her feet back on terra firma, she couldn't wait any longer to hold Billy in her arms. She just longed to feel his naked body against hers. Going up to him, she took him by the hand.

'Darling Billy, I can't wait any longer to be alone with you.'

'Wow! Follow me,' he responded, with his eyes sparkling.

He took her through the hall, picking up a bottle of champagne and two glasses on the way, down some passages that ended at a spiral staircase. Up the staircase and then to an incredible, panelled room that was, obviously, at the top of a turret. Matching the panelling was heavy oak furniture and an enormous four-poster bed.

There were vast leather armchairs, Regimental pictures on the walls, and a thick tufted red carpet covered the floor. It was a rich, luxurious, masculine room.

'I didn't see this room when you showed me round the castle.'

'No, this is my room, and I wanted to keep it for a very special occasion, and this is it.'

Putting the glasses down, he filled them with champagne, and then took something from his pocket.

It was a small leather box which he opened and held out to Caroline. Inside was a magnificent solitaire diamond ring. Caroline gasped at its size and brilliance as Billy took it out and slipped it on her engagement finger.

'There you are, darling, you can't escape me now.' Then he took her in his arms and kissed her passionately. She felt as if she was floating in heaven. 'I love you so much it hurts.' Then grinning down at her, he continued, 'Do you really love me, or is it just lust?'

'Both, my dearest, darling Billy, but at the moment lust is getting the upper hand—please, please do something about it,' she panted.

When they lay naked together in the vast bed. She desperately wanted him. She wanted to feel him inside her again. It seemed an age since they'd last made love.

She wanted their bodies to merge as one. She hung onto him with her arms and legs, holding him as closely as she could. Her mind spiralled, her body jumped as her eyes opened wide and she let out a long moan of ecstasy, that turned into a gasping sigh.

Caroline woke up to the glimmer of dawn, and for a second, she was terrified as she thought she was back on the hillside beyond San Francisco. Then she remembered where she was. She was not in the awful touch-and-go situation; she was alone with Billy, in the warm security of his enormous bed.

She felt almost overwhelmed as a great surge of joy, and happiness, swept through her.

Reaching out she stroked and caressed Billy as he lay there half asleep, half awake. As his body stirred and responded to her touch, she moved over and sank onto him, and they embraced, whispering sweet, loving endearments to one another.

Her heart bursting with joy, Caroline knew with certainty what she wanted—to be with Billy from now until the end of time.